"What a fun read! I really enjoy Mr. Harris's direct connections to the reader and the magic tricks shared throughout." —Scott

"I think the book had some great messages about honesty, the value of friendship, and how magic can be everywhere if we just look for it and don't confine its definition to mean spells coming out of a wand." —Eden

"Children's books in which the adults don't have all the answers and children are treated as interesting and competent and creative are always a hit with me. Add in Neil Patrick Harris's humor and I cannot wait for the rest of the series to come out!" —Megan

"Great book! The topic was catching and the storyline keeps you entertained! Nice touch adding the magic tricks along the way. Very inclusive book! Love it! Waiting for the next!" —Carolina

"I love the feeling of belonging that this book is filled with and would recommend everyone read this book." —Laurie

"Between the narrator and the diverse character cast, Harris created a modern Lemony Snicket. No one character is the same and the narrator himself is a character of his own." —Ally

"I love this book! Smart and charming, just like NPH. It's engaging, heartwarming, exciting, and fun! It's not condescending, but has a great message. LOVE IT."
—Zeebee

The MAGIC MISFITS

By Neil Patrick Harris
& Alec Azam

<small>STORY ARTISTRY BY LISSY MARLIN</small>
<small>HOW-TO MAGIC ART BY KYLE HILTON</small>

Little, Brown and Company
New York Boston

Text and illustrations copyright © 2017 by Neil Patrick Harris.
Story illustrations by Lissy Marlin. How-To illustrations by Kyle Hilton.
Excerpt from *The Magic Misfits, The Second Story* Copyright @ 2018 by Neil Patrick Harris

Cover art by Lissy Marlin. Cover design by Karina Granda.
Cover art copyright © 2017 by Neil Patrick Harris.
Cover copyright © 2017 by Hachette Book Group, Inc.

Little, Brown and Company
Hachette Book Group
1290 Avenue of the Americas, New York, NY 10104
Visit us at LBYR.com

Originally published in hardcover and ebook by Little, Brown and Company in November 2017
First Trade Paperback Edition: September 2018

Little, Brown and Company is a division of Hachette Book Group, Inc.
The Little, Brown name and logo are trademarks of Hachette Book Group, Inc.

The publisher is not responsible for websites (or their content)
that are not owned by the publisher.

Library of Congress Cataloging-in-Publication Data

Names: Harris, Neil Patrick, 1973– author. | Marlin, Lissy, illustrator. Title: The magic misfits / by Neil Patrick Harris ; artistry by Lissy Marlin. Description: First edition. New York : Little, Brown and Company, 2017. | Series: Magic misfits ; 1 Summary: "Six young magicians and illusionists team up to save their small town from a crooked carnival owner and his goons" Provided by publisher.

Identifiers: LCCN 2017004840| ISBN 9780316391825 (hardcover)
ISBN 9780316534581 (Scholastic)
ISBN 9780316355599 (library edition ebook)

Subjects: | CYAC: Magic tricks—Fiction. | Orphans—Fiction. | Carnivals—Fiction.
Robbers and outlaws—Fiction. | Conduct of life—Fiction. | Humorous stories.

Classification: LCC PZ7.1.H3747 Mag 2017 | DDC [Fic]—dc23

LC record available at https://lccn.loc.gov/2017004840

ISBNs: 978-0-316-35557-5 (pbk.), 978-0-316-35558-2 (ebook)

Printed in the United States of America

LSC-C

Printing 13, 2020

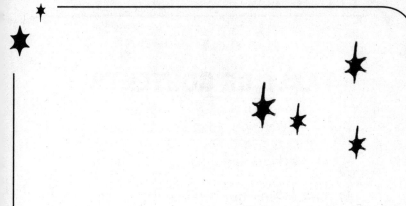

To Gideon and Harper,
who misfit together perfectly

TABLE OF CONTENTS

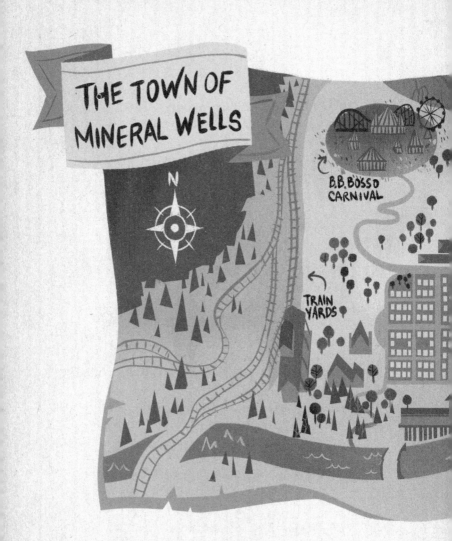

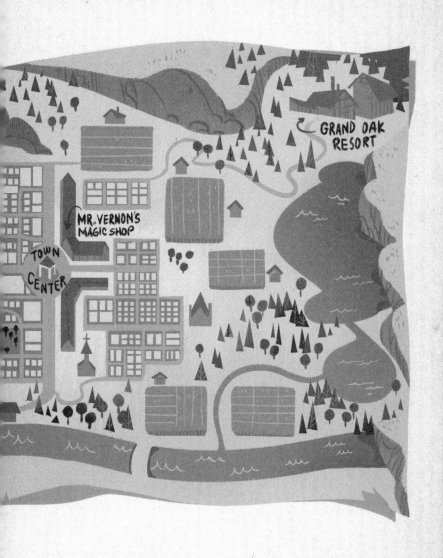

— SALUTATIONS!* —

(* This is just a clever word for "Greetings!")

Do you believe in magic? Hi there. Yes, I'm talking to you. Well, do you? Do you believe in magic?

If you're anything like the boy in this book, you might say no. But I assure you, there is magic all around you. It's true. Don't believe me? Look into my eyes and tell me you don't see magic!

iiiiiiiiiiiiiiiiiiiiiiiiiiiiiiiiiiiiiiiiiiiiiiiiiiiiiiiiiiiiiiiiiiiiiiii
iiimiiiiiiiiiiiaiiiiiiiiiiiiiigiiiiiiiiiiiiiiiiiiiiiiiiiiiciiii
iiiiiiiiiiiiiiiiiiiiiiiiiiiiiiiiiiiiiiiiiiiiiiiiiiiiiiiiiiiiiiiiiiiiiiii

See what *I* did there? Eyes...*i*'s...

(You can stop laughing. *I* wasn't that funny, was *I*?)

But let's be serious for a moment.

Magic can mean different things to different people. For some, it is pulling a rabbit from a top hat or sawing a person in half and then (hopefully) putting them back together again. For others, magic is a crisp autumn's day or a tender hug from a loved one. For me, magic can be a story, a game, a puzzle, or a surprise that takes my breath away in a single, furious gulp.

You see, magic comes in all shapes and sizes and colors and tastes and smells and feelings. Magic may even come in the shape of a book—perhaps the very one you're holding now. Or not. I don't want to get ahead of myself.

But sometimes you might have a hard time remembering to seek out the magic in the world, just like the boy in this book. You might be too busy twirling cotton candy or too distracted by birds sitting on the windowsill or too tired from organizing the attic to notice—but I assure you, magic *does* exist. You just have to know where to look. (Use your nose! Or your tongue! Or your eyes! Or your brain!) Of course, sometimes you can make it happen yourself.

Would *you* like to learn about magic? I thought you

might. Very well. Repeat after me: *SIM SALA BAM!*

I'm sorry—I don't think you actually said that out loud. Please. Repeat. After. Me: *SIM SALA BAM!*

Louder. *SIM SALA BAM!*

Brilliant. You're proving to be a good student.

Now turn the page....

WAIT, WAIT, WAIT...HOLD ON...STOP!

Silly me. *I* think *I* must have mesmerized myself with all those *i*'s earlier. *I* almost forgot one last vital thing before we get into the meat and potatoes of our magical story. (Drumroll, please!) First, *I* must explain....

HOW TO...

Read This Book!

i cannot tell you wHen or where to read this book. after all, you might rEad it on a bus or in a plane or in the back of a haY cart. you mighT read it while brushing your teetH, or brushing your hair, or brushing the fur of your angora rabbit. (you havE one of those, right?) you might Read it in a bed, under a bed, or possibly while levitating several feet above a bed. if you're so inclined, you might rEad it in a bathroom mirror backward or upside down, or down side up.

no, i can't tell you when or where—and i certainly can't tell you how. you may read it with your eyes open, or you may read it with your eyes closed (there is a way to do that, you know). you might read it backward or in a mirror, or you might have someone read it aloud to you. you might even find it helpful to read the last letters of certain words in a phrase. there is at least one part where you'll want to find all the capital letters in a section to see what they say. (nice to have options, isn't it?)

mosT important, you sHould understand that withIn thiS Book are lessOns on magic (sOmetimes spelled magicK with a k). readIng the chapterS will give you a tale of adventure and woe and excitement and Fun (not necessarily In that order). reading the magic moments (or those sections hidden here and there) wiLL aid you in uncovering the secrets of stage performance.

if you read both types of chapters in ordEr, you may finD yourself saying "woW!" as you discover an adventure and learn magic. for the most fun, mIght i suggesT reading the book botH ways?

now, magicianS' sECrets must be shared if they are to be passed on so futuRe genEraTionS cAn accomplish eveN more amazing feats and Dares. this is why i am sharing them with you! but i have A request: keep the secrets secret. no sHaring wIth your frienDs or friends of frienDs. no using them to cheat your neighbors. no shouting them from the rooftops of your town. trust me whEn i say that turNing a frown into a smile mighT be tHe most rewardING magic trick of them all. much mOre Rewarding than the opposite!

bah—listen to me blaTHering on.... let's dive in.

are you REady?

brilliant.

turn the pagE....

— — —   — — — — —!   — — — —
— — — —   — —   — — — — — —
— — — —   — — — — — — —
— — —   —   — — — — — —
— — — — —   — —   — — — — — —....

ONE

In the darkness of a train yard, somewhere on the far edge of town, a shadowy figure emerged from a thick curtain of fog. The person looked back once before dashing alongside several rows of empty train tracks.

Now, if you're anything like me, you might flinch when imagining a shadowy figure emerging from a nighttime fog in a nearly abandoned train yard lit only by distant streetlights. But you needn't worry here. It was merely a skinny boy named Carter Locke.

If you *were* to worry about anyone at this moment, it should be the man who was not far behind—the man who was chasing Carter through the train yard, bellowing: "Carter! Get back here! Don't you run from me, boy! I ain't going to hurt you!" This was a lie. The man very much intended to hurt Carter.

Thankfully, Carter knew it. So he pumped his legs and clutched his satchel and strained through the murk to see which line of cars was *chug-chug-chugging* down the tracks and out of the yard. The wail of a horn blasted Carter's eardrums, and he stumbled across a rail.

Several rows away, there came a familiar metal clanking. A rusty but colorful chain of cars clacked by, catching speed and whisking away the mist. Carter could see clearly now. He jumped over the tracks and raced to keep up with the moving train. From down the yard, the cars kept coming and coming and coming. Red, blue, green, yellow, purple, redder, black, orange, redder still.

The colorful train reminded Carter of the first magic trick he'd ever seen: a gentle hand coming close to his face and pulling a red silk handkerchief from his ear, which was tied to a yellow one, which was tied to a blue one, which was tied to a green one, and so on, and so on, and on and on. It was one of the few memories Carter had of his own father.

Instinctively, Carter touched his satchel, as if to make sure the small wooden box was still inside. It was.

Carter ran alongside the train, eyeing each passing car for a place to board. Behind him, footsteps sounded in the gravel. Then a gruff, cruel voice rang out. "Carter! Don't you dare hop on that train!" The clanging and banging did not drown out the man, who sounded closer now than before—almost directly behind him. "I've got eyes and ears in every town between here and Timbuktu! You'll never escape! Hear me? *Never!*"

Carter tried not to think about what would happen if the man caught him. Instead, he focused on the locomotive. Light glinted off the heavy wheels below as they rolled upon the tracks. The problem with trains is that they are made of metal and each car weighs a literal ton, if not more. Once they're moving, they move quickly. If Carter got too close—if he tripped—it would all be over.

A bright yellow train car was now edging past him. *Yellow* reminded Carter of a bird he once saw locked up in a cage in the window of a pet store. Weren't birds designed to fly free? Carter took it as a sign that this was the one to reach for, the one that would take him far away from here. Its ladder was just out of reach.

Jumping a train in motion may have been hard or even scary for some—but Carter had done it so many times, it came as naturally as plucking a coin from behind someone's ear or shuffling a deck of cards with only one hand.

Unfortunately, the man who was chasing Carter found it easy too. As Carter was about to clasp the ladder, the man grabbed Carter's satchel and dragged him to the ground.

"No!" Carter yelled.

They both tumbled across the gravel, rolling beside the wheels of the yellow car that went *bump-bump, bump-bump-bump, bump-bump, bump-bump-bump* over the rickety tracks, echoing the flutter of Carter's panicked heartbeat. He didn't want to imagine what would happen if the train left without him.

So Carter didn't stop moving. He twisted his body until the rolling turned into a somersault. As he pitched himself forward, head over heels, Carter yanked his bag away from the man's grip, planted his feet on the shifting gravel, then leapt toward the train's last car. A ladder hung down from the rear, next to an open door. Carter's fast hands grabbed the bottom rung, his taut tendons holding him tight. Climbing up and onto the ladder, he pulled his feet up and clung to the back of the now-racing train.

After catching his breath, he moved all the way to the top, taking a seat on the car's roof. The wind whipped his hair around. The train's horn cried out again from up ahead.

Looking back, he saw the man kneeling by the tracks, arms raised in anger, screaming into the night and quickly shrinking into a dot that eventually disappeared in the murky distance. Carter waved good-bye.

To the town. To Ms. Zalewski. And to the man who was chasing him—though if it had been possible to wish the man a *bad-bye*, Carter would certainly have done that instead.

The sky turned a beautiful blue as the sun came up. After some time, the familiar rocking and loud metal-churning of the train calmed Carter's heart and brought a yawn to his jaw. So he climbed down and into the train car. Inside, hundreds of boxes were stacked on wooden pallets. Plopping himself on the floor beside one such stack, Carter placed his satchel underneath his head like a pillow, then drifted off to sleep, dreaming about hope and fate and destiny and adventure, as well as a fleeting thought or two about the possibility of magic.

TWO

Surprise! It's time for a little flashback!

I understand how frustrating it is to pause a story right in the middle of the action, but there are a few things you should know about Carter before I tell you what happens next. Things like: Who is this kid? And why was he running? And who is the man he was running from? I promise we'll get back to Carter's escape soon enough. And if we don't, I'll let you lock me up in a tight straitjacket with no key. Oh, the horror!

But anyway...onward!

✦ ✦ ✦

Carter learned how to do magic tricks from his uncle. And they were just that: *tricks*. There was no magic involved. How could there be? Everyone knows there is no such thing as magic—or so Carter believed.

At a very early age, Carter stopped trusting in wonderful, happy, fantastic things. It wasn't his fault. Sometimes bad things happen to good people.

You see, Carter was born to two lovely people. His mom had a smile that shone like the sun on a perfect day at the beach. And his dad could pull coins out of ears and make a deck of playing cards vanish into thin air. They all lived in a tiny red cottage with white trim on a wooded and winding road outside a small northern city. One afternoon when Carter was only a few years old, both of his parents failed to come home.

They also failed to come home the next day. Or the day after that. When the babysitter called the police, Carter hoped it was only one of his father's tricks. But after another day passed with no word, Carter had to face the cold hard truth: His parents were not coming back. It was their final vanishing act.

Young Carter was taken in by a distant relative

named Sylvester "Sly" Beaton. For the sake of convenience, we will call him Carter's uncle.

Uncle Sly was a wiry little man who always dressed in a brown tweed suit with frayed seams and patches that covered moth-eaten holes. He wore his long, greasy hair tied back in a messy ponytail, and the whiskers of his patchy beard barely covered his pointy chin. Uncle Sly told people he got his nickname because he was like a fox, but Carter always thought that his uncle looked more like a weasel, which made sense because Uncle Sly often acted like a weasel too.

The man was not thrilled to have to look after Carter. And Carter was not thrilled to live with this weasel. But that's what the circumstances were, and so Carter made the best of them.

Like Carter's father, Uncle Sly knew magic tricks. He could hold a tissue up to Carter's nose and make him sneeze a waterfall of coins into a glass. Then, one by one, Uncle Sly would make the coins disappear again. This blew Carter's mind—well, his mind *and* his nose.

Carter begged his uncle to show him how to do magic. Eventually, Uncle Sly saw that there might be a benefit in having an assistant, and so he taught Carter everything he knew. It turned out Carter was a natural-born magician.

Soon enough, Carter was doing all of Uncle Sly's tricks—only better. Carter had a special talent. His fingers were long and his tendons were taut, which gave him fast hands and expert card-shuffling skills. He could make coins vanish and reappear across the room. He could materialize playing cards out of thin air. He even revised Uncle Sly's sneeze trick, using ice cubes instead of coins (which was rather impressive, given the size of the average human nostril).

Now, Uncle Sly wasn't the type of man to celebrate his young nephew's ability to change up his oldest and best illusion, but he was smart enough to notice an opportunity when it was sneezing ice cubes right in front of him. So on Carter's birthday, instead of throwing him a party, Uncle Sly decided to test him. He sent the boy up to a random couple on the street to perform his very first show.

As Carter approached, he nervously slicked his blond mop of hair to the side, pinched his pale cheeks, and opened his blue eyes wide. The couple seemed happy to stop for him. First, Carter presented a deck of cards and asked the woman to choose one and keep

it hidden between her two hands, making sure not to show him.

"Now, hold on to it tight," he said, "while I guess which card you picked....Is it the queen of diamonds?"

"It is! It is!" the woman gasped. But when she opened her hands to look, she yelped, "The card is gone!"

"Is it?" Carter asked, holding it up in his own hand.

"How did you do that?" the man asked.

"With magic, of course," Carter said, though the words were just words. Carter didn't believe in real magic, but he knew a thing or two about making people pay attention to one thing while he distracted them from something else. Growing bolder, he added, "Now, would you mind giving me back the card *you've* taken, sir?"

"I didn't take a card," the man said.

"Then what is that in your pocket?"

The man reached into his breast pocket, and sure enough, the king of diamonds was inside.

The couple laughed. With a flick of his wrist, Carter produced a bouquet of colorful paper flowers. He presented it to the woman, then took a bow, just like Uncle Sly had taught him. The couple clapped and clapped and clapped.

The lady kissed Carter on his cheek. The man gave him a nickel. Carter's proud uncle shook both their hands before hustling Carter away.

Carter beamed like the sun. He had brought joy to the young couple. In earning their smiles, he recalled his own two parents and their laughter. He didn't care that there was no party. It was still a very good birthday....

At least until later, when Carter realized his uncle had stolen the man's wristwatch and the woman's wedding ring. Uncle Sly had *used* him. Carter knew too many stories in which villains stole from innocent people. These stories always made him feel as if someone had stolen his parents from him.

What was left of that earlier, good feeling squeezed out of him like a balloon with a leak in it.

Uncle Sly was not an ideal guardian by any stretch of the imagination. Quite the opposite. You already know that he was a thief, but you should also understand that he was a con artist—someone who cheats others by getting them to believe something that isn't true.

Carter's uncle enjoyed "short cons." This means he didn't go in for long-term scams that took days or weeks to pull off. He did it as quickly as possible, robbing money or valuables off people in the blink of an eye. By the time they realized they'd been robbed, Uncle Sly was gone.

This was the reason why Carter never had a home. He'd never had friends or his own bedroom. He'd never gone to school or had a place that made him feel safe. He and his uncle slept in shelters on good days and in dark alleys on bad ones, constantly moving from town to town to town. After all, when you're in the habit of making other people's things vanish, it's best that you know how to vanish too.

Sometimes Uncle Sly even disappeared for days at a time, leaving Carter behind. Carter wouldn't know where his uncle had gone, if he was hurt or in trouble, or if he'd ever see him again. Yet Uncle Sly would always come back without a word of explanation. Carter knew better than to ask where he'd been, especially with the cruel and angry glint in Uncle Sly's eye, along with the scrapes and bruises that told their own story.

Left alone, Carter would practice his tricks, or find the closest library. He loved to lose himself in books about ideas like hope and strength and wonder, but also about things like train engineers, gymnastics, and pie recipes. Over time, he became good at fending for himself. He also became an expert cartwheeler and dreamer of sugary treats.

As the years went by, Carter's patience began to wear down. His uncle was a crook—Carter knew that. Yet he kept hoping that Sly would suddenly pick a town, get a job, and settle down. Perhaps it was a slim hope, maybe even an impossible hope, but hope was one of the few things Carter had in his possession. At least until a particularly brisk spring night...

"See that man over there?" Uncle Sly whispered to Carter. "I want you to go over and nick his watch." The word *nick*, while usually a man's name, can also mean steal.

"How many times have I told you?" Carter said. "I don't steal." He'd come up with this rule years ago when he'd figured out what his uncle really did. He promised himself that he'd never be like his uncle. No matter what. It had been Carter's code ever since.

"You little—" Uncle Sly growled as he grabbed Carter roughly by his shirt. A cop appeared, walking down the street, twirling his baton. Uncle Sly put on a bright smile and hugged Carter close, like a valued son. "—ball of sunshine! Oh, good evening, Officer."

The officer nodded and kept walking.

When the cop was out of sight, Uncle Sly took Carter by the collar and snarled, "Fine. Then keep a lookout while *I* work."

Carter's uncle's idea of *work* wasn't typical. He didn't invent the Hula-hoop or operate heavy machinery. He didn't grow rhubarb on a farm or train zoo snakes to not bite children. Uncle Sly's idea of work was a con artist's version of work: stealing from others.

Carter's fingers rubbed over the rectangular shape in the side of his leather satchel. All that he owned fit into this bag. It contained a deck of playing cards, three cups, three coins (one of which had a deep scratch down its face), some marbles, an extra pair of socks, a rope, his newsboy cap, and a small wooden box with the initials LWL on it. The box appeared to be sealed shut with no way to open it, but Carter didn't care. It was the only thing he had left of his parents.

"I'd rather just go back to the halfway home," Carter whispered to Uncle Sly. "My stomach doesn't feel good."

"It's called a halfway *house*," Uncle Sly snapped. "I won't have you acting all sentimental-like. That kind of thinking can be dangerous for folks like us. Now, pull up your britches and get ready to help me out, would ya?"

Carter swallowed a groan as Uncle Sly searched the street for a victim. Minutes later, the cop reappeared, strolling slowly, looking inside shopwindows. Carter whistled, a signal telling his uncle to stop whatever criminal act he was doing. As the officer moved around the corner, Carter looked left and right for any others on patrol. When the coast was clear, he gave Uncle Sly a nod.

Uncle Sly ducked into the mouth of an alleyway and spoke to strangers who were passing by. "Hey, check this out—see how easy it is to win? Step right up, I have an easy enough game for you. Double your money in a single minute. It's as easy as one-two-three!" The strangers must have liked hearing the word *easy* so many times, because they stopped at Uncle Sly's folding table.

Carter preferred Uncle Sly while he worked. When his uncle ran a racket—not a racket for playing tennis, mind you, but another way of saying *tricking someone*—he shone as brightly as a million-watt lightbulb. He became funny and charming and quick as electricity. His smile made old women blush, angry men applaud, and crabby babies ready to hand over all their lollipops.

When Carter's uncle wasn't working, his eyes went cold and dark. Being around him then was like walking around in a pitch-black room full of hard edges. Take a wrong step and you would stub your toe so badly it'd make you cry. Carter tiptoed a lot.

"Step right up, ladies and gents," Uncle Sly called from the alley. "I've got a game that'll knock your socks off!"

"If he doesn't *steal* your socks first," Carter grumbled to himself. As his uncle worked, the sun began to set and an unexpected chill crept over Carter. Though it was almost summer and the trees in a nearby park displayed green and glorious foliage, clouds blocked the sun, and Carter shivered. He would have pulled a scarf or a jacket out of his bag, but sadly, he didn't own either.

Since he had to keep watch anyway, Carter studied his uncle's hand movements. Uncle Sly had fast hands (though Carter knew his own were faster), and his preferred method of conning people out of their money was something called the shell game.

It involved three nutshells turned upside down on a table. Uncle Sly would place a dried pea on the table before hiding it under one of the shells. Then he'd ask the game contestants to watch as he moved the shells about. When Uncle Sly stopped, the player guessed which shell held the pea.

"That looks easy," said another passerby. "I'll give it a go."

"Most excellent, sir." Uncle Sly placed the pea on the table, covered it with a shell, then placed the other two shells on either side. "Place your bet first. That's right, set your dollar on the table. Now, keep your eyes on the shell with the pea." He moved the shells around the table, mixing them up. The passerby's eyes were locked on the shell he thought had the pea.

"Okay, pick a shell, good sir," Uncle Sly said to the passerby.

"It's this one," he said. "I know it is. I didn't take my eyes off it."

"Interesting choice." Uncle Sly smiled. He held his breath before the reveal.

Carter shook his head. The players were never right—not unless Uncle Sly wanted them to be. This was because he had the pea stashed behind the crook of his fingers. It was all sleight of hand—a magician skill that means using your hands quickly to move objects without anyone noticing. Carter knew sleight of hand to be a very useful skill for any magician. Most magicians would use it to pull a coin from an ear or plant a card in someone's pocket—all to earn smiles. But his uncle didn't use it to make people happy—he and other crooks would use sleight of hand to take things from them without their knowledge.

As Uncle Sly pulled back the shell, there was no pea. "I'm sorry, sir. You lost. Would you like to try again?"

"I never took my eyes off the shell," the passerby growled.

"I'm sorry, but it seems you did," Uncle Sly said, flashing a smile at the man. But the charm wasn't working.

Maybe it was that this man reminded Carter of his father or maybe it was simply that he had finally seen his uncle dupe a victim one too many times, but Carter knew he'd be no better than Uncle Sly if he stood by and watched it happen again.

So Carter came out from behind the corner where he'd been hiding. His uncle's eyes grew wide as Carter strolled up to the table. "It's a neat trick, isn't it?" he asked the passerby.

"What are you doing, boy?" Uncle Sly snarled, his jaw tightening, a vein popping out of his forehead.

"*Helping*," Carter whispered. Uncle Sly blinked as if his anger had made him go momentarily deaf.

The passerby grabbed the other two shells and flipped them over. There was no pea. "You no-good, dirty cheat!" he shouted.

Uncle Sly grabbed his money and the shells and dodged the man's swinging fists. Then Uncle Sly turned and ran up the alley as fast as he could. Carter took off down the street in the opposite direction, his satchel bouncing against his side.

Behind them, the man shouted, "Police! That man's a thief! Someone get him!"

This wasn't the first time Carter had to outrun the law. But it was the part he hated most. He hadn't done anything wrong—at least not to the passerby—yet if he were caught, he would still be guilty by association. So he ran.

One day soon, he thought, *I'm going to stop running. Maybe not today. Maybe not tomorrow. But soon. I'm going to stop running, settle down, and live somewhere safe.*

If he weren't so out of breath, Carter could have laughed. No matter what he hoped, as long as he was with Uncle Sly, he'd never have what he wanted most in the world: a home.

Carter walked the long way back to the halfway house where he and his uncle were staying. Looking over his shoulder, he passed through alleys, took weird turns, then backtracked, retracing his steps to see if the cops had followed. He felt nervous to face his uncle again.

A harsh wind whooshed through his clothes and brushed at the satchel hanging from his shoulder. He found Uncle Sly sitting on the steps. When Uncle Sly noticed Carter approaching, he stood up and puffed out his chest like an angry ape. Carter flinched, expecting the worst. But to his surprise, his uncle said nothing, staring at him silently instead. This was scarier to Carter than whenever his uncle screamed at him—it was so unexpected. Uncle Sly turned away, letting the door almost slam in Carter's face. Carter followed, closed the door gently, and took off his shoes. His uncle left a trail of muddy footprints in the hallway. Carter cleaned them up.

"Cold night, isn't it?" asked Ms. Zalewski in her thick Polish accent. The always-smiling old woman volunteered in the kitchen, feeding those that came through the shelter. She wore a dirty blue apron and a small, sparkly diamond on a chain around her neck.

"You look hungry. Would you like me to make you dinner?" she asked.

"No, I'm good," Carter said. He wasn't hungry, even though he hadn't eaten since breakfast.

"Rubbish," she said. "A growing boy must always eat. Come, sit down. I'll make you a grilled cheese and radish sandwich."

"Grilled cheese and radish sounds perfect," Carter admitted.

You see, Ms. Zalewski made a mean grilled cheese and radish. *Mean* is usually bad, but in this circumstance, it means extremely delicious. Carter sat at the table in Ms. Zalewski's quiet kitchen, enjoying the warmest, meltiest, crunchiest, and *meanest* sandwich he'd ever tasted. The woman's outrageous stories and her smile often warmed Carter with laughter, even after a horrible day out "working" with his uncle.

It was rare that anyone ever greeted Carter with such kindness, and he'd grown fond of her. She made him wonder about his grandparents and what a life with them might have been like.

"Would you like some prune juice, dearie? I mix it with this delicious orange powder when my pipes are clogged."

"I think my pipes are good." Carter giggled. Uncle Sly would never have talked with him about his pipes, and if he had, he'd never have tolerated Carter giggling about them.

Carter cleared Ms. Zalewski's table and washed the dishes as she told him a tale about her childhood in Poland and Russia and then coming to America by boat. "The boat was filled with good people, and crooks too. This diamond I wear belonged to my mother, and her mother before her, and her mother before her. When I came over, I hid it in a *matryoshka* doll. You know, the Russian ones with a doll within a doll within a doll. This tiny diamond is all I have left to remind me of home."

"*I used to have a home,*" Carter whispered.

"What's that, dearie?"

Carter shook his head and said nothing. He liked when Ms. Zalewski spoke of *home*. He didn't care if Uncle Sly thought he was being *sentimental*. Carter often wondered what having a real home again might feel like. Certainly it would it be better than a new bed in a new town every other week.

Uncle Sly stormed into the kitchen. He sat down and put on his famous fake smile for Ms. Zalewski.

"Can I have some warm soup and a cup of coffee, sweetheart?"

"Of course, dear," Ms. Zalewski said, disappearing down into the cellar. "Let me go get some more coffee beans."

As soon as she was out of earshot, Uncle Sly leaned in to Carter and whispered, "Today was a mess, so I need you to step up. You're gonna swipe the old broad's diamond."

"I don't steal," Carter said. "And she's not an *old broad*. She's our friend. She's been feeding us all week."

"We don't have friends," his uncle spat. "Haven't I taught you anything?!"

"Nothing good," Carter whispered.

"What was that?" Uncle Sly growled. He grabbed Carter's arm, his nails digging in. But he quickly let go as Ms. Zalewski returned with a tin can. "Aww, thanks, sweetheart," he said to her. "You're the absolute tops."

Uncle Sly put on quite a show for people when he wanted something. His earnest-looking smiles and overstuffed compliments fooled most people. Carter could see through it. Unfortunately, Ms. Zalewski ate it up, grinning as she brewed Sly's coffee.

It made Carter ill to think how easily his uncle tricked people. Like magic, smiles can warm a person's heart—but they can also be used to hide something dark and frightening.

Later that night, squeaking door hinges startled Carter out of sleep, and he woke on the cold wooden floor of their single room. Though it was still dark, he watched his uncle plop down beside him, admiring a small, sparkly diamond at the end of a thin chain necklace. Carter recognized it immediately. It belonged to Ms. Zalewski.

Carter felt sick. A rage in his stomach grew until he

could no longer contain it. Before he could stop himself, he was shouting, "Why did you take that? It's one thing to trick people in shell games, but it's another to steal something so important from someone who is nice to us. Ms. Zalewski doesn't deserve this. She's a good person. You don't care about anyone but yourself!"

Uncle Sly slipped the necklace into his pocket before flashing across the room and shoving Carter into the wall. "I raised you, took care of you, taught you everything I know, and this is how you repay me?" his uncle seethed through sour breath. "If you think you can do better on your own, go ahead. You think you're such a good person now—just wait until your belly rumbles and you're so hungry you can't see. You'll be stealing more than necklaces in no time."

"No, I won't," Carter shouted back. He pushed his uncle away, grabbed his satchel, and ran out of the room. He was halfway down the stairs before he opened his hand to see Ms. Zalewski's diamond necklace. He had lifted it from his uncle's pocket, the way his uncle had lifted it from Ms. Zalewski's neck.

Uncle Sly wasn't the only one who was good at sleight of hand.

When Carter ran into the kitchen, he found Ms. Zalewski awake and frantic. "Oh, Carter!" she said. "I think I lost my family diamond. It must have happened before I went to bed. Could you help me look?"

"I just found it in the hallway," Carter lied. "Here it is."

Ms. Zalewski was so relieved, tears formed at the edges of her eyes. "Let me get you some milk and cookies."

"I can't," Carter said, choking back a surge of emotion. "I'm kind of in a rush."

"A rush to where?" asked Ms. Zalewski. "It's still dark out."

Carter ignored the question. "Take care of yourself—and watch my uncle. He has sticky fingers." He made a bouquet of paper flowers appear out of his sleeve and handed it to the kind old woman, who only stared at him in shock.

Then Carter pulled off his first solo vanishing act: He ran away.

And that, my friend, is how Carter ended up in a train yard running *away* from a terrible man and *toward* a new—and hopefully better—life.

THREE

Many hours after hopping onto the multicolored train, Carter woke to find that it had already stopped. Panicked, he gathered his belongings. Experience told him that a conductor or a cop would eventually go from train car to train car looking for extra passengers. It was best if he wasn't caught. He didn't want to end up in a foster home, or worse—reunited with Uncle Sly.

He cracked open the metal door to see where fate had taken him. Outside, a lush green forest stretched like a fuzzy rug all the way to a mountain range in the not-far distance. The sun had just fallen behind the horizon, turning the few wispy clouds overhead a lovely fuchsia as the dome of blue sky darkened into evening. He'd been asleep for a long time.

A sign standing along a nearby road said: WELCOME TO MINERAL WELLS.

Carter climbed back up the ladder to get a better view of the town. From the top of the train car, he could see a quiet community blanketed with twinkling lights that were spread out to the north and east of the tracks. Far beyond the grid of streets, a sprawling set of buildings sat on a hill overlooking the town,

a glow coming from within the windows as if they were illuminated by the light of a billion fireflies. Closer to the train yard, across the wide gravel lot and just west of the twinkling town, was an enormous fairground where the bright lights of a traveling circus were just beginning to blink on. Colorful sounds came in waves—even from here, Carter could hear laughter and music and shrieks of excitement.

He was about to hop down when a small red car pulled into the gravel lot. Carter ducked, flattening his body against the roof of the train. It would be bad if anyone reported seeing him.

For a moment, Carter thought he was imagining things. People dressed as clowns began to hop out of the tiny red car, one after another, until a dozen different-shaped men and women were huddled in a tight group of polka dots and stripes, staring toward a lone black train car parked on its own track. Instead of a smile, each of the clowns wore a painted frown on his or her face. Each had a bag in hand.

Carter shuddered. He was *not* a fan of clowns. Whenever he'd seen them in advertisements or books, their fake expressions made him think of his uncle.

The clowns made their way to a lone train car with a giant man's face painted on its side. Big and round, as if it might just pop off the wall and roll around like a runaway boulder. The face held a creepy smile; either that or it was smirking a dastardly grin. Over his head were five letters spelling BOSSO.

The first frown clown unlocked the door of the train car. The rest began to load the bags inside the metal car. From this angle, Carter couldn't see inside. He wasn't sure what they were carrying, but he had a feeling it wasn't something good. He knew the body language of someone who felt guilty. Their shoulders were hunched and they moved jerkily, as if they were about to jump out of their skin.

"There's no more room!" one of the clowns whined. "What do we do now?"

"Up to the boss man," another clown said. "He'll probably wanna move most of the goods over to the Grand Oak Resort. Let's bolt before the coppers show."

Carter wondered if the gloriously lit buildings on that far hill were the resort they were talking about. The compound certainly *looked* grand.

Before he knew it, all of the frown clowns had

squeezed back into their impossibly small car and driven away. Carter didn't know what that was about. And honestly? He didn't care. One thing he'd learned growing up on the street was to mind his own business.

What he *did* care about was the police showing up. So Carter climbed down from the roof and made his way across the gravel parking lot toward the manic carnival lights, where he knew he could blend into the crowds.

Whenever Uncle Sly had dragged Carter to a new town, they'd always followed a strict series of rules. First, scope the surroundings. Second, find food. Third, a bed. Finally, Uncle Sly would seek out some victims so that he could get to *work* as soon as possible.

As a violent rumble shook his stomach, these rules flew out of Carter's mind. Ms. Zalewski's grilled cheese and radish sandwich was the last food he'd eaten, and painful hunger pangs were making him suddenly dizzy. The breeze carried scents of fried dough and pit barbecue and boiled sweets across the gravel lot, motivating Carter to move faster.

When he bent down to check how much of his

emergency money was left in his shoe, he gasped in horror. The stash was gone! Memories of yesterday flickered through his brain like film images in a clunky old projector. Had Uncle Sly anticipated that Carter might run away and stolen his stash in advance? Or maybe Carter had been so upset about Ms. Zalewski's diamond, he'd forgotten to remove his money from his pillowcase and shove it back into his shoe as he had done every morning since he could remember? Whatever happened, it didn't matter now. He was broke.

As Carter approached the source of laughter and music and jovial shrieking, his senses were quickly overwhelmed, which was a good thing. It gave him something to concentrate on other than his empty stomach and his swimmy vision.

Bright lights spun around the Ferris wheel and merry-go-round. Stage lights lit the red-and-white tents. Young couples lined up for cotton candy and shows, while children called to their parents for more tickets. Games cried out: *rat-a-bang-clang* and *ding-ding-dang!*

"We have ourselves a winner!" someone shouted with glee. Dozens of other voices said, "Better luck next time!"

Carter strolled beneath a giant sign that read:

WELCOME TO B. B. BOSSO'S CARNIVAL SPECTACULAR!

Bosso! That was the name from the metal car in the train yard. The puzzle pieces were starting to fit. The clowns in the tiny car were probably dropping off stuff from the carnival. Costumes. Wigs. Juggling pins. Jars filled with leftover ketchup. But why keep that train car so far from the rest of the carnival?

It didn't matter. Carter knew the best way to make it to tomorrow was to keep walking.

The smell of fried grease grew stronger, and the ground became sticky wherever he stepped. Carter's stomach roared. The salty and sweet aromas mixing in the air made his mouth water. Something that Uncle Sly said zipped back into his brain: *Just wait until your belly rumbles and you're so hungry you can't see. You'll be stealing more than necklaces in no time.* What if Uncle Sly had been right?

With no money, nothing to eat, and a growing sense of desperation, Carter wondered how he'd keep himself from breaking his code that very evening. He could have easily used his talents to acquire some carnival tickets, but he didn't steal, which included tricking people into giving him something for nothing. However, if he fainted, someone might call the cops.

"*Welcome, one and all, to the greatest show this side of the Appalachian Trail!*" a sideshow barker echoed through a cone from the top of his podium. The thin man looked like a stick figure, yet his voice boomed like he was a giant.

"Play games, win prizes! Eat food 'til you're sick. Hear the hysterics within Cuckoo's Fun House! Get lost in the Mind-Bending Maze of Mirrors. Shudder in the shadow of Bosso's Blender, the most thrilling thrill ride since the last time you threw up! And make sure you stick around at the end of the night for Bosso's Grand Finale Show!"

Strings of lights glimmered overhead. People streamed by Carter, burbling with shouts and laughter. A burly carnival worker in suspenders swung a sledgehammer down on the base of a machine that said

TEST YOUR STRENGTH, and a bullet-like capsule shot up and rang the bell.

"Step right up!" The burly man pointed the sledge-hammer at Carter. "Are you a man or a mouse?"

"Neither," said Carter. "Sorry, I don't have any money." He was too embarrassed to tell the burly man how hungry he was. "But maybe I could help you, and you could buy me a corn dog or something?"

The burly man looked annoyed. He nodded at another man in a stiff-looking dark blue security uni-form. As the guard came closer, Carter noticed that his face was painted like one of the frown clowns from the tiny car in the train yard. He was even freakier looking than an ordinary clown.

Yikes, Carter thought. *Time to vanish again!*

"See the Sickest Sideshowers on Earth!" a woman in an ill-fitting jacket and a bowler hat cried from nearby. "Wonder at the Walrus, a brute who lifts weights with his mustache! Watch the Spider-Lady weave her weirdo web! Feed nails to the Tattooed Baby! Torment your-self by talking to the Two-Headed Woman!"

There didn't appear to be any admission fee to this tent, so Carter ducked inside. He followed a group of spectators through a dimly lit gallery lined with glass boxes: a half chicken, half pig; the world's longest fin-gernail; a Venus flytrap whose bulb was the size of a cracked watermelon. Last was a glass coffin containing the skeleton of a mermaid.

As others oohed and aahed, Carter rolled his eyes. All these things were fake. He could see the seam where the chicken and the pig had been joined together, as well as the wood grain in the fingernail and dried paint on the Venus flytrap. One of the mermaid bones even had a price tag still on it.

A large velvet curtain gave way to another room, this one separated into a series of small stages, one after the other. Carter looked over his shoulder, but he didn't see the security clown following him any-more. Maybe he was safe now?

He began to lose himself in the strange surroundings.

The first stage featured a plump toddler in a diaper whose skin was covered in tattoos. He sat in the middle of an enormous wooden playpen, giggling, drooling, and banging some blocks together.

"When is he going to eat some nails?" a spectator near Carter complained. The Tattooed Baby glared at the man, spit at the ground, then went back to banging blocks harder than before.

"Someone needs a diaper change," Carter whispered to himself.

The next stage was completely black except for a giant silvery web strung from the front to the backdrop. On the web lounged a woman with a small, pale face and impossibly thin limbs, clad all in black. Carter did a double take when he realized she had two extra sets of arms extending from her sides. With a bored look, the Spider-Lady was painting her nails in fire-engine red polish, holding the bottle in her toes and the teeny brush in one of her mid-hands.

Thinking of some of his own tricks, Carter looked more closely. The extra arms were covered in the sleeves of her black sequined dress, but the hands were bare. The fingers didn't move. *It's fake*, Carter thought. *They're all fake.* Since there wasn't an admission fee, technically they weren't breaking Carter's Code; still, it didn't seem fair to the audience. It seemed like something Uncle Sly would be a part of.

The next stage held an enormous glass aquarium, several feet wide, several feet long, and taller than the tallest man Carter had ever seen. He thought it was strange that there was no water in it. The glass was filthy and could barely be seen through. As people pushed their faces against it, they screamed or gasped. One woman nearly fainted. When it was Carter's turn, he saw why. Inside sat the Two-Headed Woman calmly reading a book. The distorted view made her even more ghastly.

Carter spit on his sleeve to wipe away an inch of dirt so he could see better. *Of course the glass is so dirty*, Carter thought. *The sideshow needs the audience's view to be blurred.* Inside, he saw one neck naturally joined, while the other wobbled awkwardly. The first face moved and blinked, while the other stared blankly. It was a mannequin head attached to a real person. *More tricks*, Carter thought. Part of him was relieved, the other part disappointed.

A third part gurgled again with hunger.

Carter blushed and then glanced around to see if any of the other spectators had heard him. There was still no sign of security, so he proceeded to the fourth and final display. This stage buckled under the weight of the heavy objects upon it—a diesel engine, an anvil, a refrigerator, and an upright piano. Center stage, a hairy-chested hulk of a man flexed his muscles. His ropy handlebar mustache hung down past his chest. This was the Walrus. He squatted in front of an iron bar with what looked like cannonballs on either end, each labeled 500 LBS. The tips of his mustache were tied to the giant weight.

With a roar as fierce as a lion's, the man struggled to stand, the barbell swinging at his waist. The downward pull on his mustache disfigured his face into a ghoulish grimace. His nostrils flared. Carter couldn't help but laugh. When the man brought the barbell to the ground, Carter saw that the man was staring at him with dark, piercing eyes.

Carter headed out of the tent, returning to the night air. He noticed others walking about mystified or horrified or astounded by what they'd seen. He managed to smirk to himself. People shouldn't believe everything they see. It's one of the first rules of magic.

Carter knew that.

Do you? A quick lesson: While showing you one thing (perhaps with a right hand), a magician will often be doing another thing that you don't notice (probably with his left). This is called *misdirection*. It was one of the first things Carter had learned from Uncle Sly.

B. B. Bosso's two-bit sideshow only reaffirmed Carter's belief that there was no such thing as *real* magic.

Yet at this precise moment, something truly magical happened to Carter that he couldn't explain. Something that would change his life forever.

He met Mr. Dante Vernon.

FOUR

Have you ever been so captivated by a sight that you have literally been unable to turn away? Maybe it was a sunset that filled the sky with spatters of color just as the moon rose over the horizon. Or maybe a rare animal somewhere out in the wild fearlessly approached you to make sure you were friendly. Or maybe it was a musician who was able to play five different instruments all at once. For Carter, seeing Mr. Vernon in the midst of the crowded carnival was *just that spectacular*.

The man wore a black-and-white suit, with his sleeves rolled up at the elbows. A cape hung from his shoulders, black on the outside and shiny red on the inside. His head was crowned with a top hat, floating on a cloud of white curls, which contrasted against his pitch-black mustache.

Yet it wasn't merely the outfit that caught Carter's eye. It was what the stranger was doing with a coin.

The quarter rolled across his knuckles, back and forth. But each time it got to the edge of his hand, it vanished, reappearing at the other side instantaneously.

The wheels and cogs in Carter's mind spun, trying to figure out how the old man did the trick. But he couldn't. For a moment, he wondered if his eyes were fooling him. Had his empty stomach made him so weak?

"How'd you do that?" Carter finally asked.

"Magic, of course," the old man said.

Carter shook his head. "There's no such thing." He knew that he sounded confident, but inside, for the first time ever, he quaked with doubt. There was something special about this man. Carter couldn't turn away.

"I disagree," the man said. "Magic is all around us. We just have to pay attention."

"Yeah, okay," Carter scoffed. "If you're referring to the carnival, I can guarantee you it's all fake. Just like the sideshow. Just like the games." He knew he should leave—find some food, find a bed. But something in his gut kept his feet planted to the ground. It was a similar feeling to watching Uncle Sly disappear as the train pulled away—like this meeting was meant to be.

Have you ever felt like that? It's as close to a magical feeling as some of us will ever get.

The man's eyebrows rose. "How intriguing. Do tell."

"See that game over there? With the metal milk bottles and the baseball?" Carter pointed. "My theory is that it's a con. Secret wires must hold the bottles in place, so even if you get a direct hit, they don't fall down."

"I saw someone win just a moment ago," the man noted.

"They have to do that every once in a while," Carter explained. "If no one ever won, people would catch on. But if they let someone win every half hour or so, no one picks up on the fact that everyone else loses."

"Aren't you observant?" the man said, impressed. "I take it you're *not* enjoying the carnival?"

"I didn't really come here to enjoy things," Carter said. He'd come here to vanish. "But then I saw your coin trick." He looked more closely at the man's fingers. "Are there two coins?"

"There are, actually. Color me impressed." The man with curly white hair extended his hand. "My name is Mr. Vernon."

When Carter shook it, the hand came loose and fell to the ground. Carter jumped back. It took him a full two seconds to realize the hand was made of lifelike plastic. Unable to stop himself, an uncontrollable laugh escaped. The laugh surprised Carter. He quickly corrected himself. "You got me. So what are you selling?"

"Selling?" Mr. Vernon asked, confused.

"No one does magic just for fun. Either you're here to swindle people or you're trying to sell something."

"I assure you, I'm here to do neither. But that is a rather sad view of the world for someone your age," Mr. Vernon said. "Might I ask, what happened to your youthful naïveté, Mister…"

"The name's Carter. And I have no clue what you just said."

"I was asking about *innocence*, young man. Most people start out with at least a dollop."

"Let's just say I've been around the block a few times. Sorry to bother you. I'll let you get back to your *work*, whatever it is…."

It hurt Carter's heart to step away from this strange man in the top hat, but he knew he had to. A shriek erupted from down the midway as someone on one of the rides got a little too excited. The sound sent creepers up Carter's spine. "I really gotta go."

Mr. Vernon quickly added, "It was nice to meet you, Carter. Before you run off, may I ask, where are you visiting from?"

"How do you know I'm not from here?" Carter asked.

Mr. Vernon's bright grin flickered briefly. "Aha. A worthy question. Well, in a small town like this, everyone knows everyone. You'd know that if you actually *were* from here." He tossed up an apologetic shrug and the inside of his cape flashed satiny red. "Considering our mutual appreciation for magic, I'd like to think that if you did live here, we'd know each other."

"When you say magic, you mean tricks," Carter said. "Right?"

"I mean what I say, and I say what I mean." Mr. Vernon smiled. "Is it safe to assume you have a few tricks up your own sleeves?"

"I do," Carter said. He held his hands out flat, palms down. He turned them up to show his hands were empty. He turned them down, then up again. This time, Mr. Vernon's pocket watch was in Carter's palm.

"Bravo!" Mr. Vernon said. "You have fast hands."

"That's what I've been told."

"Of course, so do I." Mr. Vernon pushed his cape back to reveal Carter's satchel. He handed it back to Carter.

A rush of anger flew over Carter as he felt at the satchel to make sure the wooden box was still in there. It was.

"How did you do that? It was around my neck. I didn't feel a thing—" Carter shook his head. "So are you a thief?"

"I am not," said Mr. Vernon. "Are you?"

"I never steal," Carter growled.

"Then we are the same," Mr. Vernon said. "I take it you've had a rough start at life."

"That's none of your business," Carter said, scoffing.

"You are absolutely correct. I apologize," Mr. Vernon said. He offered a small bow. When he straightened himself, his face was rather serious. "Carter, let me share a bit of advice. Despite the shine of this place"—the magician held up his hands to indicate the whole carnival—"there are some very dark elements at work here. If they knew of your talents, they would certainly try to take advantage of you, to make you think the way they do. I advise you not to give in. Instead? Trust your instincts. They will serve you well in ways you've yet to witness but, I assure you, you are closer than you think."

Mr. Vernon paused, then presented a warm smile. "But the decisions you make are yours. Don't let me tell you what to do. After all, you know me as well as you know the rest of Mineral Wells." He sniffed and then added darkly, "Which is to say: *Not at all*." Producing a deck of cards at his fingertips, Mr. Vernon said, "I must be going. But I'll leave you with a card trick, if you like." Carter couldn't say no. "Take a card, any card."

The cards sprang out of Mr. Vernon's hands and shot toward Carter like machine-gun bullets. Carter raised his arms to swat away and shield himself from the rapid-fire onslaught of the card storm. When the last of them fluttered to the ground, Carter realized he held a single playing card.

It was an ace of spades with a giant letter *V* inside the spade in the center of the card.

"What's this for?" he asked.

But the mysterious Mr. Vernon was nowhere to be seen.

FIVE

Mr. Vernon had vanished, and Carter was still so hungry he worried that he soon might vanish too. This time, for good. Leaning against a wooden fence at the edge of the fairground, his stomach growled. He tried to think of something else.

He had a dozen questions for the odd Mr. Vernon, the least of which was how he managed to disappear in a flash of cards. The man with curly white hair was the opposite of his uncle in every way. Mr. Vernon's smile was genuine. He did tricks for no reason other than to be friendly. And his cryptic warning made it seem like he cared more about Carter's well-being after a two-minute chat than Uncle Sly had shown in a lifetime.

Carter flipped Mr. Vernon's ace card over and over in his hand, wishing he knew how to find the man again. Finally, he slipped it into his sleeve for safekeeping. (He had a hidden pocket stitched into his sleeve for certain tricks. It always seemed to come in handy. Well, sleight-of-handy!)

In the colossal red-and-white tent at the center of the carnival, Bosso's Grand Finale Show finally finished with a flourish of trumpets. The sky had turned fully black, its stars sparkling in the night like a mirror image of the little town below. As people came out of the tent, smiling and laughing and discussing the amazing feats they'd seen, Carter felt lonelier than ever. He'd been waiting a long time to get away from Uncle Sly, but he had never expected to feel so nervous. Everyone exiting the big top was with loved ones. As they passed through the exit, the crowd separated into clumps of friends and families bound for their homes.

He imagined walking toward one of the twinkling lights in the sleepy town. Once there, he'd find a cozy bed, a warm fire in the fireplace, and, most important of all, someone to say good night to him. His eyes burned. None of that would ever happen. It was far more likely that he'd be sawed in half and magically put back together.

Nobody in the crowd even noticed Carter sitting alone on the wooden fence. His stomach let out another long growl. When he saw a family toss their leftovers into the trash, his stomach grumbled even louder. While Carter didn't like eating out of a trash can, it wouldn't be the first time. Free food was often too hard to pass up.

Like everything else, there was a craft to it. You didn't go after food touching the sides of the can. You also didn't eat anything that was covered in flies. But if something was uneaten or still wrapped up—then bingo! *Bon appétit!*

However, this is probably not the best idea for anyone outside of Carter's dire circumstances.

Carter peered into the metal barrel. He pulled out a bag half full of popcorn, a B-shaped pretzel, and an untouched corn dog still warm in its foil wrapper. He even found a sealed bag with half a stick of cotton candy left. Jackpot! This was today's dinner and tomorrow's breakfast.

He tucked the pretzel into his satchel. Sitting behind the big top, he devoured the corn dog and popcorn. He was licking cotton candy dust from his fingers when two massive hands grabbed him from behind.

"Gotcha!" said a deep voice.

"Let me go!" Carter cried, struggling to free himself. It was the mustached sideshow strongman. He was so strong, Carter couldn't escape his grip. *Maybe those were real five-hundred-pound weights*, Carter thought.

The Walrus tossed him over his shoulder and walked toward the edge of the fairgrounds. "I said, *let me go!*" Carter shouted.

"Shut your trap," the Walrus snarled. For all of Carter's skill, he wasn't a trained escape artist. He couldn't get out of the strongman's iron grip. He wrenched his eyes around, crying out in vain for help. The fairgrounds had emptied. No one was there to hear him.

On the far side of the big-top tent, away from the stringed lights, a black-and-gold-striped trailer stood alone. The crew had wheeled it down from one of the circus's train cars up at the yard. The Walrus climbed the steps with Carter still struggling to escape, beating on the strongman's back. The brutish Walrus knocked on the door and said, "*Bahzooley bahzooley*." A lock released and a frown clown swung open the metal door.

(In case you were wondering: the word *bahzooley* is a nonsense word. But sometimes nonsense words can be used as passwords to open doors to secret places. Try inventing your own. It should be as nonsensical as possible so no one can accidentally guess it. See how many *x*'s, *y*'s, and *z*'s you can fit in!)

The Walrus plopped Carter onto his feet, and the boy gaped in awe. The inside of the trailer was like a palace, with a crystal chandelier hanging from the ceiling. Golden lamps adorned the polished oak walls, and Persian rugs covered the floor. A small blond monkey in a red fez sat on top of a shelf, winding a crank on a small box that played calliope music.

The Spider-Lady was draped over a maroon sofa against one wall. In this lighting, Carter could see that her extra sets of arms had almost-invisible wires connecting them to her real arms. She brought a long black cigarette holder to her red lips and blew out a stream of smoke.

Nearby, the Tattooed Baby sat not in a playpen but instead at a desk with a scale, an adding machine, and a mountain of wallets, watches, and jewels. His alphabet blocks were nowhere to be seen. After the Baby examined each item, he scribbled a note in a ledger and placed them in large bags. Each bag had a zipper and a padlock to keep it secure. He wasn't a baby at all, Carter realized. He was just a very small man doing actual *adult* work!

Shocking, I know. And Carter barely managed to tear his gaze away.

On a raised platform, a very *large* man was tilted back in a crimson barber's chair. His face was hidden by a steaming white towel, but Carter's eyes were dazzled by a bright green emerald ring sparkling on the man's left pinky finger.

Atop a stool beside him, a short frown clown stood, carefully shaving the man's neck with a straight razor. The clown hummed "Oh My Darling, Clementine." It sent a cold chill up Carter's spine.

The Walrus directed Carter into the center of the room, followed by the security clown. The strongman kept him in place with one hand gripped around the boy's neck. No one spoke.

The short clown on the platform wiped the last of the shaving lotion off the man's face with the towel, jumped off the stool, and pulled a lever on the side of the chair with a grunt. As the chair swung upright, Carter came face-to-face with a balding man whose smile was crooked. Wide nostrils, as big as the holes in bowling balls, seemed to sniff at Carter. The man was huge, as wide as he was tall, and his presence just as big. Two green eyes seemed to stare straight through Carter, as if they could read his mind.

Carter recognized him from the painting on the side of the train car. This must be B. B. Bosso.

"What'dya want, Walrus?" the carnival owner barked. "And what's with the kid?"

The Walrus nodded to the security clown at his side. "Your guard here told me to bring him in. He was eating out of our trash."

"No, I wasn't!" Carter lied.

Bosso snapped his fingers and a cigar appeared at his fingertips, his emerald ring glinting alongside it. He puffed on the cigar's tip, and it lit all by itself. He leaned forward, his big belly blowing up like a balloon, and then released a cloud of smoke into Carter's face.

"You a thief?"

"No! I never steal," Carter growled. He pushed

down his fear and pulled up some courage. "I found
a corn dog and some popcorn in the trash. Someone
threw it out. So what?"

"So you *were* stealing from me," Bosso said.

"No one owns trash," Carter said.

"If it's in *my* carnival, it's *MINE*!" Bosso shouted,
slamming his fist onto the chair arm. The monkey stopped winding the music box and screamed at
Carter too.

"Check his pock-
ets," Bosso said,
"and his bag."

Carter tried
to resist, but the
Walrus's hand
kept him in place as
the frown clown searched
him. "Nothing in his pockets, Bosso. The satchel only
has a bunch of junk. Oh, and that trash he took."

"Not a thief, huh?" Bosso said. "Tell me, son. Have
you been grateful for my hospitality? Free shows, free
food...Perhaps you'd like the ring off my finger?"

Bosso dangled the bright emerald ring in Carter's
face. Carter didn't say anything. A knot formed in his
stomach, growing tighter by the minute.

"You better let me go. I need to get home," Carter
lied. "My parents are probably looking for me."

"Your parents?" Bosso laughed. "Kid, I know a
street rat when I see one. If your parents are outside,
my name is Aunt Petunia."

The Spider-Lady, the Tattooed Baby, the Walrus,
even the clown, all joined in on the laughter. Everyone was laughing except Carter.

Bosso pointed at the security clown. "Spike, what's the big idea bringing this kid in here? I know it wasn't purely for my amusement."

The clown perked up. "I had my eye on him ever since he came down from the train yard. But then he just vanished. Every time I thought I saw him, he vanished again. The kid's got talent...*talent we could use*."

Bosso's eyes went wide. He stared at Carter for several seconds as if he'd stumbled upon a stone that might actually be a precious jewel. "Look, *friend*," Bosso said, changing the tone in his voice to warm and smooth—the same way Uncle Sly did when he wanted something. "I know plenty o' people like you. No family. No friends. No place to go. Maybe they feel a little bit like *misfits*. So you know what I do? I give 'em jobs. I give 'em purpose. Now they're all happy to work for me."

Carter glanced around the room. The sideshow performers nodded; the frowning security clown smiled. Everyone in the room kept reminding him of his uncle in some way.

Bosso continued. "You don't have to be on your own anymore. Come work with me. You'll have a family, you'll travel the world, you'll even get a percentage of our earnings. All you gotta do is join my crew—but of course, if you cross me, I'll throw you in front of a train." Bosso released a terrifying bellow of laughter, as if he'd just invented the funniest joke he'd ever heard. "What'dya say?"

Carter felt torn. He'd been so hungry earlier, he'd almost considered breaking his code. The idea of a roof over his head—even a traveling one—was still more than he'd ever had. Sure, Bosso was gruff and imposing, but his offer seemed like a real option with real money involved.

"Come on, kid. Sorry I grabbed you so hard. Say yeah. It ain't such a bad life," the Walrus said. The strongman smiled, revealing half his teeth were missing.

The Spider-Lady lit another cigarette and purred, "We can be the family you've always dreamed of...."

When he got nervous, Carter played with his sleeves. As he reached up to touch them, he felt Mr. Vernon's ace of spades. He recalled Vernon's warning.

Carter didn't want to trade his uncle for more con artists. He knew instantly he had to get out of there.

"It's not a bad offer," Carter lied again. He even smiled and waggled his eyebrows, doing his best impression of Uncle Sly. "Can I think about it?"

"Absolutely," Bosso said with a wide grin. "But don't think too long. We're only here for two more nights, staying at the Grand Oak Resort up on the hill. Otherwise, you can find me here. The door is always open. Unless it's locked. Then don't bother me. Hope to see you soon...*friend*."

Bosso's crooked mouth curled into the scariest, phoniest smile Carter had ever seen.

The Walrus opened the door. With Bosso still grinning, Carter forced himself to walk slowly out into the fresh night air, to pretend he was calm and collected. But he wasn't. A wave of fear had risen up inside him. As soon as the caboose door closed, Carter ran as fast and as far as he could, and then threw up.

HOW TO...

Roll Coins on Your Knuckles!

Oh, hello there! So sorry to interrupt. You were probably expecting further tales of Carter. They'll continue right after this brief magical interruption. You may skip ahead if you like (I won't take offense)...OR...you could stay a moment and learn a bit of magic to impress your family, your friends, and your pets. (Yes, animals like magic too.)

You might be thinking the magic tricks in this book are impossible for you to learn. But you're wrong. Learning magic is not a trick at all—it's a skill! Magic is like learning to ride a bike or play the piano. It's not hard to learn, but mastering the best parts are a matter of *practice, practice,* and *more practice*.

That means if you work hard at it then you too can be as good as Mr. Vernon when it comes to coin skills. I'll give you the basics. Perhaps your parents can give you the coin?

WHAT YOU NEED:

Your hands and fingers
A large coin (Start with a quarter.)

HELPFUL HINTS (ORDER OF FINGERS):

Thumb
Index finger
Middle finger
Ring finger
Pinky

STEPS:

1. Hold your hand out,
   palm facing down.

2. Take a coin and place
   it on top of your
   middle finger.

3. Lift your index finger until it is above the coin. (You can also lower the middle finger to help!)

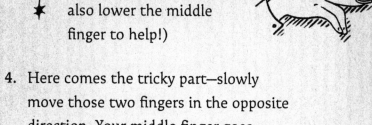

4. Here comes the tricky part—slowly move those two fingers in the opposite direction. Your middle finger goes up, while your index finger goes down. It should catch the edge of the coin, making the coin flip over from the middle finger to the index finger.

Hurrah! You did it! If you didn't, that's okay. *Mistakes are part of mastery.* Try again. It's tricky!

5. Now, keep doing this, over and over and over and over and over again. Once you have mastered it and can do it fast or slow, try moving the coin from the index finger to the middle finger to the ring finger.

6. Got it? Now add in the pinky finger.

7. Hard, isn't it? But don't give up. As all magicians know, practice makes perfect.

Remember: *Practice, practice, and more practice.* (And then practice again. And after that, practice a little *more.* Then take a nap, wake up, have a snack, and get back to practicing. All this work pays off. I should know. . . . Once upon a time, I was just like you!)

ADVANCED STEP:

1. Want to go a little further? Then try this: Use your thumb to cross underneath your palm and grab the coin from your pinky.

 2. Now move the coin back to your index finger and start again!

If you practice this enough and get really good at it, it will make the coin appear to vanish and reappear back at the start each time. *Voilà!*

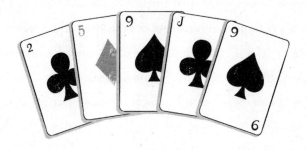

SIX

The next morning, Carter woke up on the bench in front of the town hall where he'd spent the night. Someone had covered him with a bristly old blanket. He felt for his bag across his chest. Still there, thank goodness.

His vision spun as he took in the park across the street, to see if anyone might be watching him. Its crisp green grass reached out for several blocks in either direction. A grand-looking white gazebo stood directly in the center of the lawn. Quaint, colorful buildings lined the streets that surrounded the park.

Whimsical wooden signs hung over doors to shops that weren't yet open. There was one shaped like a tall boot, another like a striped piece of red-and-white candy, and another was an old-fashioned silver key. The area was empty except for a few well-dressed people out for a morning stroll, and no one looked in his direction.

He was relieved to see the sun. Not having a home was always hardest when it was raining. Carter got up, stretched, then peed behind some bushes. Something jangled inside his pants pocket. Reaching inside, Carter pulled out several coins. They must have come from the same person who'd covered him with the blanket. But who? Then he remembered: the circus crew. They'd probably followed him and were trying to convince him to join them. Unsure of who gave him the blanket, Carter folded it and stashed it beneath the bench in case he needed it again that night.

He was about to throw away the B-shaped pretzel from the previous night, but then he thought better of it and tore it into pieces, sharing most of it with a crowd of pigeons before taking a few bites for himself. At least some good came out of that horrible man.

Without Uncle Sly making the daily decisions, Carter wasn't sure what to do next. He could choose his own fate. Should he leave town or stay? (He had no idea.) Should he join Bosso's crime circus? (Absolutely not.) Should he search for Mr. Vernon? (Where would he start?)

He took Vernon's ace card out of his sleeve and flipped it over in his hand. It was an ordinary card. But examining it closer, he noticed the tiniest crease. He held it up to the sunlight. Sure enough, there was an almost invisible fold down the center. He opened the crease and found that the ace of spades became a jack of diamonds. Except the image of the jack was holding a business card in his hand with an address on it: 1313 Main Street. "Whoa," Carter whispered.

A warm feeling rose in his chest—it was an unfamiliar sensation. It made him feel awkward and vulnerable, so he tried to push it down. Perhaps Mr. Vernon would turn out to be a nice guy. But he could just as easily turn out to be as bad as Bosso or his uncle. Either way, Carter wouldn't get his hopes up.

Carter circled the small park, found Main Street, then followed the numbers until he reached a small shop tucked between two taller office buildings. The sign over its door was shaped like a top hat. The hand-painted letters on the glass window read:

Vernon's Magic Shop
Purveyors of the Impossible

When Carter entered, a tiny bell on the door rang out loud. A green-feathered parrot with a yellow neck squawked, "Hello, Carter! Welcome to Vernon's Magic Shop!"

"How did that bird know my name?!" Carter asked, astounded.

"Magic, of course," said a large-eyed girl sitting on the counter. She wore a white jacket with straps that tied her arms behind her back.

"There's no such thing as magic," Carter said, recalling this was the same conversation he'd had with Mr. Vernon the previous night. But as he looked around the shop, he felt something hopeful stir inside.

The two-story shop's walls were covered floor to ceiling with bookshelves and autographed black-and-white photographs of famous magicians. Every surface was cluttered with magical items of every sort: crystal balls, decks of cards, top hats, wands, capes, and even a human skull. A wooden staircase curved up toward a small balcony, where there sat a small wooden table and two leather chairs. The table was empty except for a chessboard, mid-game.

Carter felt like a kid in a candy store—except hungrier. (Well, not as hungry as he was one night prior...) His gaze swept over the towering shelves packed with alphabetized boxes labeled things like FINGERTIPS, FLASH PAPER, FOG, and FOOLS' GLASS. He wanted to ask what it was all for, but he felt embarrassed, so he promised himself that the next time he found a library, he'd look these things up. There were bouquets of rainbow

feather flowers, jars filled with marbles of all sizes, a ventriloquist's dummy in a tuxedo and a cape (very much like Mr. Vernon's from the night before), even a white rabbit hopping across the floor!

"So you're Carter?" the girl said.

"Yes," Carter answered uncomfortably. He didn't like strangers knowing his name. "Um...do you need help getting out of that?"

"My straitjacket? No, thanks! I've got this. But do me a favor and count to five."

"One...two...three..."

"Forget it. I'm out!" she cried, shaking the jacket off. Underneath, she wore a formfitting black shirt and pants. She hopped down from the counter, walked confidently over to Carter, and extended her hand. "My name is Leila the Great, escape artist extraordinaire. Nice to meet you, Carter." Brown irises sparkled with flecks of amber in her eyes. Her wavy dark hair draped to the nape of her neck and bounced whenever she moved her head.

"Were you expecting me?" Carter mumbled, taken aback.

"Nope. But my dad was," Leila said.

"Who's your dad?"

"That would be me," a voice said from behind him. "I believe we've already met."

Startled, Carter nearly jumped through the window. A moment before, he and Leila (and the parrot) had been alone in the shop. He was certain of it.

"Mr. Vernon!" Carter said. "Where'd you come from?"

"Here and there," Mr. Vernon said, avoiding the question. "I see you found the store."

"So I was right. You *were* selling something," Carter said, motioning to the store. "No one does magic just for fun."

"*I* do!" Leila proclaimed.

Mr. Vernon shook his head. "I wasn't trying to sell you anything, Carter. On the contrary, I simply recognized a kindred spirit and shared something that brought a smile to your face. That's hardly a crime, is it?"

Carter's cheeks flushed as he remembered the kindness that this man had shown him at Bosso's carnival. Still, he couldn't bring himself to say thanks for the warning about Bosso, at least not in front of this girl. He was sure that she didn't need to know about his predicament.

Mr. Vernon placed his hand over a stack of the business cards and made one flutter across the counter. It floated off the surface and danced on air. A moment later, the card dropped into his hand.

Carter felt that excitement stir in his stomach. It was an unfamiliar feeling. He found himself craving more. "How'd you do that?"

"Magic," Mr. Vernon said simply.

"There's no—" Carter started.

"—such thing," Mr. Vernon finished for him. "Yes, yes, you've said as much. I respectfully disagree. Look around you. I've tried to create a sense of wonder for those who step across my threshold. Do you not feel it?"

Carter *did* feel it. But it made him uncomfortable that this stranger could read him like a book.

Nodding, Leila piped up again. "I saw his face when he walked through the door. He *definitely* feels the wonder."

Carter crossed his arms and pursed his lips.

"Still with the gruff demeanor and dark outlook, I see," Mr. Vernon said. "Very well. Not everyone need be cheerful all the time. Magic accepts all kinds. I'm happy you're here. I was just telling my daughter about you."

"How are you two related? You don't look anything

alike," Carter noted. Leila's golden-hued complexion suddenly turned pink. Carter immediately wished he could take the words back; he hadn't meant to embarrass anyone.

"Families come in all different shapes and sizes," Mr. Vernon commented as he pulled a feather duster out of nowhere and began cleaning a shelf that didn't look like it needed cleaning. "Like a snowflake or a thumbprint, no two look alike."

"Plus, I'm adopted," Leila clarified with a grin. She pulled a pair of handcuffs from the counter and locked them onto her own wrists. "But I was rather lucky ending up with someone who understands my need to escape. I was good at it before, but since I came here, my dad's taught me all sorts of ways to do it better."

"Luck? Don't you mean magic?" Mr. Vernon smiled, tugging at Leila's handcuffs to show they were on securely.

"I prefer to think of it as fate," Leila reasoned.

A spark awoke in Carter. *Fate.* That's what he'd felt had brought him to this town too. He'd sensed it while climbing to the roof of the train car, and it had only grown as his uncle disappeared into the distance.

Leila walked over to Carter and clapped her hands.

When Carter looked down, the handcuffs were on *his* wrists.

"How'd you do that?" Carter asked. He knew plenty of tricks, but already he could tell these people were experts compared to him.

"Escape artist," Leila said in a pointed whisper, "remember?"

The tiny bell on the door rang again as a bearded man with dark eyes and a handsome smile entered.

The parrot squawked, repeating, "Hello, Carter. Welcome to Vernon's Magic Shop."

Carter laughed. "So it *wasn't* magic! You just taught the bird to say that to everyone who walked in today."

Mr. Vernon shrugged, trying not to laugh. "Did I?"

"Hello, Carter," the other man said. "I'm Mr. Vernon."

Carter looked from Mr. Vernon to the second Mr. Vernon. They looked nothing alike either. The second Mr. Vernon was several inches shorter than his counterpart, and wore glasses. His trimmed beard covered the bottom half of his face, which shone in the morning light that streamed through the shop windows. He was dressed in a stained white jacket that had two rows of shiny buttons running up the front, and his pants were checkered black and white.

Seeing Carter's confusion, Leila explained, "I have two dads." She rushed over to this new man and kissed his cheek. "Hi, Poppa!"

"I don't even have one parent," Carter said. "You're lucky."

"You can call me the *Other* Mr. Vernon," Leila's second dad said to Carter. "Everyone does...well, except for Leila here. I don't do magic—except in the kitchen."

"You make food disappear?" Carter asked.

"No, he's a cook. *I'm* the one who makes food disappear," Leila said, rubbing her stomach.

"He's not simply a cook," Mr. Vernon noted. "He is the *head chef* at the Grand Oak Resort. You might have noticed it overlooking our town."

"It's a beautiful resort—usually," the Other Mr. Vernon explained. "Ever since that B. B. Bosso and his crew checked in, they've been making an absolute mess of everything. Demanding food when the kitchen is closed, raiding the pantries after hours, behaving like beasts. Those vagabonds are absolute animals."

Carter cringed at the word *vagabond*—which means a person who wanders from place to place without a home or a job. Carter had been called a vagabond—many times.

Mr. Vernon threw a harsh glance at the Other Mr. Vernon, then quickly added, "Carter, did you know that the famous illusionist P. T. Selbit grew up without a roof over his head? They say it gave him the drive to be a successful magician."

The Other Mr. Vernon ducked behind the counter, scanning the area. "Apologies, I didn't mean to interrupt, but I forgot my key. Where is that thing?"

"Is this it?" Leila asked, holding up a key at the center of a series of knots and bound rope.

"Would you mind?" the Other Mr. Vernon asked, putting his hand out.

Leila—in less than two seconds—unknotted the ropes and placed the key in her father's hand. She kept the rope for herself. Carter couldn't believe his eyes. Her hands were as fast as his own.

"Thank you very much," the Other Mr. Vernon said. He kissed his daughter on the forehead and waved politely to Carter as he stepped outside. "Nice to meet you."

"*Oooh*, this rope gives me an idea for a trick I'd like to practice!" Leila smiled.

"Brilliant. But perhaps *after* school," Mr. Vernon said. "Shouldn't you be on your way, young lady?"

Leila's confident smile slipped into a frown. "Carter's not on his way to school."

"Well, then it's a good thing that you're not Carter."

"I—I'm between schools right now," Carter blurted out.

Thankfully, Leila ignored this. "May I take the day off?" she asked her father.

"A day off from school?" Mr. Vernon raised a pointy white eyebrow. "Whatever for, my darling daughter?"

"It's been a tough week. The other kids..." Leila said quietly. "They just don't...understand me."

"If you can escape a straitjacket," said Mr. Vernon, "I'm sure you can find some way to impress one or two of your classmates. And if not, just tie them to their chairs!"

"Believe it or not, most kids *don't* like hearing about how to escape," Leila explained. "That's the problem: I offered to show them how it all works, but now none of the girls will let me sit with them at lunch! And the boys, they just laugh at me in the hallways and call me *Freak*."

"Freak?" Mr. Vernon echoed, appalled. "Maybe chivalry *is* dead."

Leila rolled her eyes. "Don't you mean, *chivalry is dumb*?"

"You could always try disappearing instead," said Carter. "That's helped me get out of tons of predicaments."

Leila laughed. "Well, I *am* in a predicament." Sighing, she added, "I'll give it a shot." She walked over to her dad and hugged him. As she passed Carter, she stuck out her hand again. "A pleasure to meet you. See you soon?"

Carter shook her hand. "I hope so."

Then Carter and Mr. Vernon were alone. Mr. Vernon continued to dust his totally clean shop. Without looking, he asked, "Tell me, Mr. Carter, how was the remainder of your evening? Uneventful, I hope?"

"Bosso tried to get me to join his gang," Carter admitted. "I said no."

"Brilliant."

"How did you know he was going to ask me?" Carter wondered out loud.

"I didn't *know*," Mr. Vernon said. "But I had a very strong *hunch*. B. B. Bosso is a greedy man. He's also something of a collector. You've got some skills that would make a fine addition to any collection."

Carter put his hands in his pockets. "You obviously don't know me very well."

"Nonsense. You are a young man with great intelligence, even greater common sense, and an honorable code for living. No matter where we live or how much we have, these are the most important things. You have quite the talent with your fast hands. In my entire career as a magician, I have only seen one other person with such nimble fingers."

Carter was stunned into silence. Did Mr. Vernon know he was homeless and poor? Or was he guessing? Carter felt undeserving of such compliments. He wondered suddenly if Mr. Vernon was the one who'd left the blanket. But how could Carter ask him without revealing the truth of his situation?

"You're wrong," Carter whispered. "I'm a...a..." He tried to think of the word Bosso had used the previous night. "A *misfit*."

"Aren't we all misfits of some sort or another?" Mr. Vernon called out, suddenly upstairs, looking over the balcony.

"How'd you—?" Carter gasped.

Mr. Vernon took a book off the shelf and dropped it down to Carter. The old orange cloth cover was embossed with black lettering: *Vanishing & Unvanishing*, by Bailey & Barnes.

"What's this?" Carter asked, cracking open the cover and flipping through the first few pages. It was slim enough to fit nicely in his bag, and yet—

"Homework," Mr. Vernon said. "Read it. I suspect you'll appreciate it."

"I don't have any money," Carter admitted.

"Consider it a gift," Mr. Vernon said with a toss of his hand. "From one magician to another."

"I'm not a magician," Carter said, his voice trembling. "I just do tricks."

"Then you don't see what I see," Mr. Vernon said. "And seeing is believing, as the saying goes."

The man hurried down the stairs and grabbed his cape and top hat from their hooks on a wall. He led Carter toward the door. "Unfortunately, I have a terribly busy day and need to close the shop while I see about a few things around town. But you should come back. Say, about four o'clock?"

"Uh, sure, I can do that," Carter said, confused. He was both grateful for the gift and surprised to be getting kicked out after such a short talk.

"Brilliant," Mr. Vernon said, pushing him out the door. "Four o'clock sharp. See you then."

SEVEN

Carter spent the warm day in the park reading the book Mr. Vernon had given him. He'd never owned a book before. As soon as he opened it, he was unable to remove his eyes from the simple black-and-white illustrations explaining magic tricks he'd once thought impossible.

He pored over the drawings and words from cover to cover. Then he began again at the beginning and started to memorize the first trick. Before he knew it, the bell in the town hall clock tower chimed four times. Looking up from the book, he discovered that

Mineral Wells had come to life. A great many people of all shapes, sizes, colors, and ages walked along Main Street. The adults were carrying shopping bags filled with clothes, and groceries, and art supplies, and antique knickknacks. The kids wandering home from school wore heavy knapsacks on their backs.

A large sign had been erected on an easel in front of the huge gazebo. It read:

B. B. BOSSO'S CARNIVAL!

IN TOWN FOR A LIMITED TIME!
BIG-TOP SHOW TONIGHT!

FINALE FANTASTIC TOMORROW AT THE GRAND OAK RESORT! SEE THE WORLD'S LARGEST DIAMOND!

Four performers, dressed in matching jackets with red-and-white vertical stripes, bow ties, and straw steamboat hats, climbed the steps up to the gazebo's platform. Three were men, and one was a woman. Though they all looked somewhat similar, each stood out from the next. One man was tall with a razor-sharp snout. Another was short with a curly mustache under a bulbous beak. The third man was medium height; his face was scruffy, and his belly spilled slightly over his belt buckle. The woman had a great big smile with teeth that flashed an almost-blinding white. Carter slipped his book into his satchel and walked over to watch.

The four singers hummed. Then, like spokes on a train, the four bobbed up and down in unison.

"Pock   pock

*   pock   pock*

pick   pick

*   pick   pick—"*

"Look, a barbershop quartet!" someone said. A circle of onlookers began to gather in front of the stage. Somehow the singers kept alternating the pock-pick rhythm the whole time they sang.

"What a town! What a town!
What a marvelous town
For a showwwwwwww!

"You have rings, you have gold,
You have fortunes untold
To blowwwwwwww!

"Hold your hats, peel your eyes,
'Cause you're in for a surprise.
One thing is for sure,
We sing now to procuuuuuuuuuuuuuuuuuuuuuure...."

Their hats raised in harmony, the four held the

note so long the crowd began to clap. In unison, the singers wheezed for breath comically before launching into a rhythmic chorus.

> *"Pock pock pock pock,*
> *Pick pick pick pick,*
> *Walk walk walk walk,*
> *Trick trick trick trick."*

Hats in their hands, the foursome descended the steps and fanned out into the crowd. They danced with a tall woman wearing a pearl bracelet. They embarrassed a shy man who held up his hands in surrender. They blew kisses at a blushing lady with gold earrings. They tweaked the nose of a beaming pigtailed girl with a lollipop.

The crowd continued clapping, many giving them the loose change from their pockets and purses. Within moments, all four singers' hats were overflowing with coins and bills.

> *"Pick pick pick pick*
> *Pock pock pock pock*
> *Quick quick quick quick*
> *Bock bock bock bock..."*

They flapped their arms and waddle-stepped like crooning chickens back to the stage, where they dumped their hats into a dirty white sack marked with a big black dollar sign.

But as Carter looked back through the crowd, his learned instinct kicked in: The tall woman no longer had her pearl bracelet. The shy man no longer had a watch. The blushing lady no longer had her earrings. And the pigtailed girl no longer had her lollipop.

The audience had been so impressed with the singing that they hadn't noticed the singers taking more than tips.

"When the Pock-Pickets come to town
You'll never guess what's going...
Dowwwwwwwwwwwwwwwn...
In!
Our!
Sensational!
Showwwwwwwwwwwwwwww!"

As part of their finale, the stripes of their jackets switched from red to black, as if somebody pulled a tab in a pop-up book. The showpeople now looked like jailbirds with their bag of money. The crowd went wild. No one would have guessed their act wasn't a joke. They *were* crooks. They had robbed the watchers blind.

Carter felt a pang in his side. But he ignored it. He didn't know these people. It was none of his business.

Was it?

"Thank you! Thank you, residents and visitors of Mineral Wells!" the Pock-Pickets cried out in unison. "Come to B. B. Bosso's Carnival and stay for his magic show at the big top at the end of the night! And if you want to be truly amazed, come to his Finale Fantastic tomorrow night at the Grand Oak Resort—where you can also see the world's largest diamond! One night only! It's not to be missed!"

Carter turned to leave when a voice from the crowd rose up.

"Wait, do not go!" A brown-skinned boy in a tuxedo with a white bow tie stepped to the front of those gathered around the stage. "Is that the end of your performance?"

"That's the spirit!" one of the Pock-Pickets said. "How 'bout an encore, gang?"

The four started snapping their fingers, but the

boy held up his hand. "Please," he said, "do not sing another note. My ears cannot take it."

Carter thought the boy was part of the act until he saw irritation and confusion flashing across the singers' faces.

Stepping on stage, the boy reached inside his pants pocket. He jiggled his hand as if looking for keys or spare coins, then produced a violin bow, far too long to have fit inside a pocket. The bow was exquisitely constructed of dark polished wood with tapered black ends and strung with a ribbon of silvery horsehair. Carter's curiosity was snagged. The boy knew stage magic too. But how did he fit that bow in his pocket?

"You wanna play something?" said the tall Pock-Picket. "Be our guest!" The foursome began to hurry off, but the boy pinned their bag of loot to the ground with his foot.

"Hey, get your own tips, kid!" the Pock-Picket with the scruffy face hissed.

"I do not want your money," the boy said. "And my name is not 'kid.' My name is Theo Stein-Meyer, and I wager that you will stay for my act." Theo's hair was short and dark, his eyes were thoughtful, and his long nose had a regal look to it.

Carter arrived in the front row just in time to see a violin slide out of Theo's tuxedo jacket and into his left hand. Carter was good at sleight of hand, but Theo's moves were astounding. He immediately wished he could watch the move again in slow motion.

Theo lifted the violin to his shoulder, rested his chin on its edge, and began to play. The money sack began to move. It seemed to dance in sync with Theo's violin music. The crowd began clapping again. Carter stared at the money bag shuffling away. It reminded him of Vernon's move that morning, making the playing card dance. But how did they do it? It wasn't magic; it had to be some kind of trick.

"There is a unique connection between each of us and our possessions," Theo said as he played, his eyes fluttering nearly shut, as if under a spell. Carter couldn't tell if the boy was acting or if he really believed what he was saying. "When a beloved object is lost, it longs to return to its owner."

The bag jerked across the stage until it leapt off and onto the ground. Theo walked after it, the spectators moving aside to let him pass. The restless bag of

loot came to attention in front of the tall woman, like a dog wanting to be pet.

"Ma'am," said Theo, playing more quietly, "have you lost something?"

The tall woman looked inside the bag and shook her head no. The crowd became confused and began to whisper. The violinist began to sweat. But Carter understood.

Theo was trying to help those who'd been robbed. But he mistakenly assumed the Pock-Pickets had placed the stolen goods in their loot bag. Carter eyed the singers, noticing a lollipop stick peeking out from a Pock-Picket's back pocket.

Carter wondered about the violinist. Why had Theo been trying to help a bunch of townspeople by foiling the pickpocketing singers? He obviously knew a little magic himself, but what was in it for him?

It's none of my concern, Carter tried to tell himself. But was that true anymore? As the crowd began to mumble and ask questions, the violinist turned pale. The Pock-Pickets started stalking toward Theo with red faces. The boy had stumbled onto the trouble that Carter had been trying to avoid.

"Keep playing!" Carter suddenly yelled, surprising

himself. He made eye contact with the boy in the tuxedo and gave him a reassuring nod. Nervously, Theo began to play again, and the sack began dancing along with it.

Carter pretended to dance, then bumped into each of the Pock-Pickets, one after the other. "Isn't this music great?" he shouted at them. The singers didn't notice what Carter was doing—he was pickpocketing the Pock-Pickets.

One Pock-Picket's pockets picked. Two Pock-Picket's pockets picked. Three Pock-Picket's pockets picked. Four Pock-Picket's pockets picked. *Say* that *four times fast*.

Go on...I'll wait.

Carter winked at Theo to keep going. Continuing to dance through the crowd, Carter bumped into the tall woman, slipping her pearl bracelet back onto her wrist, he barreled into the shy man, slipping his watch back onto his wrist, and he knocked into the pigtailed girl, plopping the lollipop back into her mouth.

Puh-lopppp!

But the earrings? Carter had no idea how earrings worked. How could he put those back on without the woman noticing?

Theo met his eyes, and both boys knew they had

an understanding. Theo danced the money bag back onto the stage, finishing out his song. "Thank you, kind audience, for allowing me to play." As he took a bow, Theo tossed his violin high into the air.

The entire crowd gasped, looking up.

As gently as possible, Carter slipped the earrings into the lady's handbag.

Theo caught the violin with ease, and everyone began to applaud.

Patting their pants, the Pock-Pickets finally realized that Theo and Carter had outsmarted—and out-pickpocketed—them. The singing quartet glared daggers at the two boys as they slunk away from the gazebo with only their bag of tips.

Theo and Carter shrugged, then burst into laughter. They were so distracted that neither noticed the slim woman dressed in a slinky black dress and a pillbox hat with a weblike veil over her face. She stared at them, her fingers twitching like spider mandibles chewing a meal.

EIGHT

"The singing thieves have been foiled," Theo said, moving away from the crowd and toward the curb. "Thanks to you."

"I was just following your lead, Theo," Carter admitted. "How'd you know what they were planning to do?"

"I had no clue," said Theo. "I was passing by, stopped to watched, and then noticed their sneaky game. If not for you, I would have made a fool of myself." He gave Carter a quick nod of gratitude. "I could have sworn they put the stolen objects in the bag. No matter. We saved the day. Since you know my name, would you mind sharing yours?"

"Carter."

"Nice to meet you, Carter. A fortunate coincidence you being here," Theo said, adjusting the cuff links on his sleeves. Then he pushed the violin bow back into the pocket of his tuxedo pants, despite it being longer than his thigh.

"How did you do that?" Carter asked. "The bow is way too long to fit in your pocket. And how did you make the money sack move?"

Theo grinned from ear to ear. "I am afraid I will not be revealing that to you just yet. Perhaps another time. But I must admit: I am impressed! You have sweet skills too!"

Carter's chest swelled. It felt like a great compliment, especially coming from a boy in a tuxedo who spoke like British royalty. "Why were you helping the people in the crowd?"

"Because they could not help themselves," Theo said. "They did not know they had been robbed."

"But what do you get out of it?" Carter asked.

"Nothing, I suppose," Theo said, "except knowing that I did what was right. That's worth something....

What is wrong? You look confused."

Carter *was* confused. Mr. Vernon used magic but wasn't selling anything. Leila used magic to escape things for fun. And Theo used magic to help others. But if experience (and Uncle Sly) had taught Carter anything, it was that others would always let him down.

Yet in these people, he felt kindred spirits. They reminded Carter of himself.

Not knowing what to say, Carter gave a wave and mumbled, "Well, nice meeting you."

"You're leaving?" a voice asked. "But we just arrived."

Carter turned to see Leila coming down the sidewalk alongside a girl in a wheelchair whose hair was red and unruly. Leila wore a smile, while the other girl gave Carter a cautious (almost annoyed) once-over.

"Carter, you know Theo?" Leila asked, surprised.

"Just met, actually," Carter answered.

"You know Leila?" Theo asked Carter.

"Small town," Leila said.

"And I'm Ridley. Ridley Larsen. Yes, I'm in a wheelchair. Don't ask me about it or you'll get a bloody nose."

"Cross my heart," Carter said, crossing his heart.

Theo squeezed Carter's shoulder. "You will never guess what just happened."

"Probably not," said Ridley. "How about you just tell us?" Theo went on to relate the tale of how Carter had helped him stop the group of criminals from robbing the crowd in the park. "You should have seen us! A perfect team!"

"That's amazing, Carter," said Leila. "Very impressive."

"Theo did most of the work," Carter added. "I was just sort of his assistant."

Just then, a group of four kids dressed in expensive-looking clothes walked past and snickered, pretending (though not really) to hide their laughter.

At the same time, Carter, Leila, Theo, and Ridley looked down at their feet and whispered, "Jerks." They all looked at one another and—at the same time—said, "They weren't laughing at *you*—they were laughing at *me*." All four chuckled and then turned toward the magic shop.

"People laugh at me because they think I'm strange," Leila explained as she led the group up the street. "I *like* being strange."

"People laugh at me because I wear a tuxedo," Theo added. "My parents got a great deal at the tuxedo emporium before I was even born!"

"People laugh at me because I'm smarter than

them," Ridley said. She flicked at a bike bell that was attached to the arm of her wheelchair. It rang out: *Ring-ring!* "It's not my fault that they don't read books."

"People laugh at me for all sorts of reasons," Carter finished. He couldn't bring himself to tell them that the reasons were his worn-out clothes and his unwashed hair and that he sometimes dug through trash cans for dinner.

They walked in silence for a bit, then Leila asked, "Who wants cookies?" She stopped in front of Vernon's Magic Shop. "My poppa made linzer tarts this morning."

Two women wearing fancy floral dresses and wide-brimmed hats swung the door open and exited the shop, pushing past the group, laughing hysterically. "What a fantastical store!" one of the women cried out. "You kids have fun in there."

"We always do," said Leila, waving the others to follow her inside.

The store parrot squawked from her perch near the register and everyone jumped. The bird repeated what sounded like an odd poem:

"Rub the Yellow Piranha for the Magicians Club! Rub the Yellow Piranha for the Magicians Club!"

"What's the Yellow Piranha?" asked Carter.

Leila shrugged. "Usually our parrot is smart. But sometimes she just says nonsense. Carter, meet Presto. Presto, meet Carter."

"Nice to meet you?" Carter said, unsure if he should offer a hand to shake. He'd never talked to a bird before.

The bird squawked again, insistent: *"Rub the Yellow Piranha for the Magicians Club!"*

"Yes, yes, Presto, my girl," said a voice near the ceiling. When Carter looked up, Mr. Vernon was standing on the balcony overhead, still holding that feather duster as if it were his magic wand. "We all heard you, crazy parrot." That seemed to be enough to calm the bird down. "Sorry, friends! She gets excited sometimes."

"*Excited* isn't the word I'd use," Leila whispered. When she waved her hand, the parrot flew over and landed on her shoulder. Leila made kissing sounds, and Presto echoed them back to her. Then they both giggled.

Ridley glanced around the store. "Where's my Top Hat?"

Carter thought it best not to ask why Ridley would keep her top hat at Vernon's Magic Shop. Theo reached underneath the counter and pulled out the white rabbit that had been hopping around the store earlier that day.

"Come here, Top Hat," Ridley cooed, a true smile spreading across her face. Theo placed the rabbit on Ridley's lap, where it nestled against her stomach, nose twitching furiously.

"Ridley's mom is allergic," Leila explained, "so we're babysitting Top Hat for her."

"The Other Mr. Vernon has been feeding her well," Mr. Vernon said. "Don't you worry, Ridley."

"I'm not worried. Not one bit."

A knowing smile appeared beneath Vernon's black mustache as he turned to Carter. "I see you've met the others."

"I did," Carter said. But his mind questioned whether the meeting was by chance or by design. Had Mr. Vernon purposely asked Carter to return at four, knowing the kids would be getting off school? "Do you three meet here a lot?" Carter asked Leila.

"Every Friday after school lets out," Leila said. "Ridley is homeschooled, Theo goes to private school, and I go to public. So we don't get to see one another except here. We meet, talk illusions and tricks, and, of course, practice."

"I practice *levitation*," Theo said, "as in, making things float in the air. You saw my work earlier today."

"I love learning about *transformation*," Ridley added. She pulled a top hat off a nearby shelf, moved it behind her wheelchair, and when it reappeared, it had become a book with a top hat on the cover. "I like to change objects from one to another."

"And I *escape*!" Leila said. "Dad, can you please chain me upside down in a tank full of water?"

"I can, and I will—when you turn eighteen," Mr. Vernon said.

Ridley turned to Carter and asked pointedly, "Do you have a skill?"

"I don't know," Carter said, blood rushing to his face. He thought of his parents disappearing. He thought of running away from Uncle Sly. "I guess you could say I make things vanish."

"I *could* say that?" Ridley asked with a smirk.

"We *should* say that," Theo finished, raising an eyebrow at her.

"Making things *vanish* is a fantastic skill for a magician," Mr. Vernon interjected. "Using a similar technique in reverse is called *production*. I suspect you're quite good at both. After all, many magical routines use a combination of those very ideas. A great magician learns to master not one but many of the various effects. For example, the classic *cup and balls* uses vanishes, productions, penetrations, transformations, and transportations."

(Friends, this is very good information to know when learning about magic. I hope you are writing it all down.)

"How long have you been practicing magic?" Carter asked.

"Since I was about your age," Mr. Vernon said. "Back then, I had a group of friends who would get together, just like these three do now."

"When I grow up, I want to be known as the first female Houdini!" Leila said.

"I will take after Harry Kellar and levitate a princess," Theo noted. "Or maybe even a queen...if I can find one."

"No one is as great as John Nevil Maskelyne," commented Ridley. "He was not only a stage magician but an inventor and a writer as well."

The three began to argue. Clearly this was an argument they had had many times before, and there would be no winner. Carter and Mr. Vernon exchanged an amused glance.

"Opinions are like hearts," Mr. Vernon said. "Everybody's got one."

"Not *everybody*," Carter answered. "I know some people who seem pretty heartless."

"Still full of doubt, I see." Vernon squinted at him. "No matter. A healthy amount of skepticism is not a bad thing. Especially when trying to make new friends."

"Friends?" Carter echoed.

"Isn't that why you're here?" Vernon asked.

Carter set his jaw. "I'm here because you told me to come back at four o'clock."

"Is that so? You *were* a little late." Up went that pointy white eyebrow. "You probably didn't notice, though, because you were so busy strolling down Main Street with this trio, who definitely *do not* want to be your new friends."

Leila, Theo, and Ridley emerged from a huddle. They were all staring at Carter. "What is it?" he asked, his voice cracking. "What did I say?"

"My vote is yes," said Theo. "He saved me."

"My vote is no," said Ridley. "He's too green."

"My vote is yes too." Leila smiled. "And my reasons are my own. Carter, we've just voted and would like to invite you to our secret hideout. Are you in?"

Carter had to hold back from shouting YES; instead he smiled and then gave a little nod.

Leila put on an upper-crusty tone and said, "Father, if you wouldn't mind turning away?"

"Of course." Mr. Vernon grinned, adding with a dramatic whisper, "One of these days *I will find* that secret hideout, and then it'll all be over for you rascally kids."

Leila chuckled as she walked toward a bookshelf at the rear of the store and pulled on a thick volume entitled *Secret Passages*. The bookshelf made a clicking sound and then moved outward to reveal a doorway to a darkened, windowless room.

"This is where Dad hides the good stuff that's not for sale," Leila said, flicking a light switch on the wall. "But we adopted it as our secret HQ."

Carter was so shocked, all words flew from his head.

Inside this new, secret room were antique reading chairs, lamps, more shelves adorned with pieces of knotted rope, elaborate heart-shaped locks with matching keys, and countless old photos of smiling people covering the walls. There was even a framed portrait of Houdini with his wrists shackled together. This was clearly Leila's space. Next to a pile of leather trunks, a tiny woodstove warmed the room. Nearby, the wall was hung with a framed picture of Leila being hugged by her two dads.

When Uncle Sly did a trick, Carter thought, it was to

gain something. But here, behind the secret door, there were no tricks. It was an invitation to be part of a group, a team, a crew. Whether that included new friends, Carter wasn't yet sure. Instinctively, his hand trailed down to his satchel. He touched the wooden box and a warm, welcoming feeling of home flooded over him. Or at least it was what Carter imagined a home to feel like. He only had vague memories of that little red cottage with white trim where he'd once lived with his parents.

"Pretty awesome, huh?" Leila asked.

"It's perfect," Carter whispered.

Leila raced up to the apartment above the shop and fetched the linzer tarts from the kitchen. When she returned, she blew a kiss to Mr. Vernon, then closed the door to the secret room. She and the others began to pore over the books and discuss future plans.

Carter simply couldn't believe it. This morning, he had woken up alone on a park bench. And now these strangers had invited him into their home and, further, into their secret place. It was amazing how a chance meeting and a few laughs could bring such different people together—it was almost like...

Carter didn't have another word for it.

It was like magic.

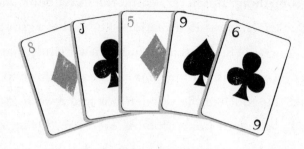

NINE

After what seemed like an eternity and yet no time at all, Ridley looked at her watch and said, "We should go."

The four had spent the last few hours in the secret room in Vernon's Magic Shop, and it was the most fun he'd ever had. Theo showed Carter how he pulled the bow from his pocket (a wire mechanism that allowed the bow to fold in half). Leila showed Carter how she escaped from handcuffs (a key hidden under a square inch of fake skin on her wrist). And Ridley showed him a secret code she had been working on, using actual cards from a playing deck.

In exchange, Carter showed them some of his card and coin tricks. Ridley kept rolling her eyes until she looked in her pockets to find an entire deck of cards stuffed inside. Then she quieted down. The Other Mr. Vernon brought them a platter of tiny cucumber and cream cheese sandwiches with all the crusts cut off. Carter wanted to shove the last few into his bag, but he knew that would look strange. He began to worry about what he'd do when Leila kicked everyone out. There was no way he could sleep on the park bench again now that he knew how close it was to the magic shop. But where else could he go? If Uncle Sly were here, they would have already worked several shell games and made at least enough to get through a couple of days in a boardinghouse. That, however, was all in the past.

"Come on," Theo said, waving for Carter to follow.

"Where?" Carter asked.

"To the carnival, silly," Leila said. "We've been looking forward to it all week."

"Oh," Carter said, feeling his stomach drop at the thought of Bosso and his goons. "I think I'm going to pass."

"Why?" Theo asked. "I thought everyone enjoyed the festivities of public revelry."

"Yeah, umm...I went last night," Carter said. "It wasn't that great. I'm pretty sure the stuff in the sideshow is fake, and the games are all rigged."

"We know that," Ridley said. "That's why we want to go—to figure out how everything works and beat them at their own game."

"It's always good for young magicians' minds to learn

all the mysteries around them," Theo added. "That way we can better replicate them."

"Come on," Leila said, taking Carter's arm in her own. "It'll be fun!" Carter didn't want to go, but he also wanted to keep hanging out with his new...*friends.* Reluctantly, he gave in.

What was the worst that could happen? (If you ever

find yourself as a character in a story, refrain from asking yourself this question. Inevitably, you will find out the answer, and most likely you will *not* like it.)

The sun had nearly set by the time they made it to the fairgrounds. As the four passed under the twinkling stringed lights at the carnival's entrance, Carter was on edge. He withdrew the newsboy cap from his bag and put it on. He pulled it low over his eyes, hoping that none of Bosso's gang would recognize him.

"Let's get some ride tickets!" Leila said, grabbing Theo and pulling him over to the ticket booth. While the others waited in line, Carter found himself alone with Ridley by the twinkling gate. Theo and Leila seemed to accept Carter without question, but Ridley looked at him like he was a machine she was trying to figure out.

"So?" Ridley asked point-blank. "What's your deal?"

"My deal?"

"Yeah, where are you from? Where do you live? Where do you go to school? Why are you here?" Ridley asked.

"It's complicated," Carter answered honestly.

"So tell me."

Carter kicked some spilled popcorn on the ground. He wasn't sure how to answer, but the silence was growing tense.

"I'll be blunt," Ridley said. "I want you to know that I don't trust you. Not one...solid...inch. I voted for you not to see the secret room. Theo and Leila see the best in people. I don't. Funny how we just spent hours together and I still don't know a single thing about you. So I'll ask one last time: Why are you here?"

"Here in Mineral Wells?" Carter asked, shaken by Ridley's aggressive questioning. Quickly, he lied, "My parents and I are staying at the Royal Spruce Hotel."

"You mean the Grand Oak Resort?"

"Of course that's what I meant," Carter answered, forcing himself to chuckle. Ridley's fierce stare was throwing him off.

"What do you want from Leila and Theo?" Ridley asked. "What do you want from Mr. Vernon?"

"Nothing," Carter said. "Nothing! I don't want anything from anyone. I never have."

"That's not true," Ridley said. "Everyone has something up their sleeve."

Dozens of thoughts rolled around in Carter's head.

He wanted a home. He wanted a family. He wanted to have friends. But none of those things were realistic. At least not until he came to Mineral Wells. Right now Carter was just trying to hold on to the happiness he'd found since meeting Mr. Vernon the previous night. But how did he say all that to Ridley or Leila or Theo without sounding like a total wastrel? *Wastrel* is another word for *vagabond*, that horrible term. The three would vanish him faster than he knew how to vanish himself!

"I'm not a bad person," he whispered.

"You didn't answer my question." Ridley's stare was unbearable. "What do you want here?"

"To belong, okay?" Carter snapped. He felt tears in his eyes, but he wasn't sure. Quickly, he wiped at them. "You don't know what it's like to be alone."

Ridley flinched. "You'd be surprised what I know."

The two stood in silence for a moment, then looked at Theo and Leila, who were laughing and smiling in the ticket line. "They have it easier than most," Ridley said quietly. "That's why they're so fast to accept others. Me? Everyone treats me like I'm different. I'm not different. Not *that* different. I'm just me." She softened. "I wasn't trying to be a jerk to you or anything. I'm just protective of my friends."

Ms. Zalewski came to mind. Carter said, "I understand. So am I."

"I guess we have more in common than I thought," Ridley admitted. "So you really want to be a magician?"

"I don't know. I've never really thought about it," Carter answered. "What magic I did just seemed to cause others pain. But watching you all, it seems cool. And I am good with my hands."

"Oh yeah? You wouldn't know *real magic* if it ran over your toes." With a grin, Ridley ran over Carter's foot with her wheelchair.

"Ow!" he said. For a moment, he thought Ridley had broken their unspoken truce. Then he noticed the words REAL MAGIC had appeared on the top of his shoe, the letters composed of tiny pieces of masking tape. Carter laughed in amazement. "That's really good! You'll have to teach me that one."

Ridley finally smiled. "We'll see."

Theo returned to the gate with Leila holding a stack of small blue paper tickets. She said, "First I want to ride the spinning swings, then we should do bumper cars, and then we have to ride Bosso's Blender. I heard it'll make you puke out of your ears."

"And that's fun how?" Theo asked.

"How is that *not* fun?" She laughed and then pulled out a pair of handcuffs from her pocket, slapping them quickly onto Theo's and Ridley's wrists before pulling them toward the swings.

"You go ahead," Carter said. "I, uh…didn't get any tickets." He couldn't afford to. But then he remembered: *Someone* had made coins appear in his pocket just that morning.

Would it be worth buying his own tickets instead of using the money for dinner? No, it was better to save the money for a real emergency.

"We purchased enough for all of us," Theo said, awkwardly maneuvering his handcuffed arm to hand Carter some of his. "Leila, can you please remove these?" Leila smacked her palms against their wrists, and the cuffs released. "Thank you."

"No, really. It's fine," Carter protested. He felt uncomfortable taking the tickets without giving something in return. "I'm not sure I even want—"

"You're riding the rides with us," Theo interrupted. "No *ifs*, *ands*, or *buts*."

Carter worried that if he didn't accept the offer, they'd think he was hiding something. And though he *was* hiding something—many things, in fact—he wasn't ready to risk losing anyone over it.

As the swings lifted into the air, and the bumper cars crashed into one another, and the Blender spun them in nauseating circles, Carter forgot himself. The newsboy hat that he'd pulled low over his brow was working. This was the first time in a very long while that he'd allowed himself to feel somewhat safe.

Afterward, the gang walked along the aisle of game booths. They each took turns trying to figure out how the games were fixed—*fixed* in this case means set up to be advantageous to one person, and it wasn't the person playing the game.

At the Milk Bottle Pyramid, Carter offered up the theory he'd told Mr. Vernon. Ridley added, "Probably. But they also could fill the bottoms with lead so they weigh, like, ten pounds each. And look—that heavy curtain behind them helps hold them up."

At the Balloon Dart Throw, Theo said, "They underinflate the balloons, and the darts are too light to have any force behind them. So they bounce right off."

At the Duck Pond Game, Leila noted, "Catching the rubber ducks with the pole and string and hook is easy, but ninety-nine percent of them have a lame prize marked on the bottom. No one wins the big prize here."

Ridley appeared to be the sharpest of the bunch. As she rolled down the strip, she'd point and say, "That basketball hoop is too small for the ball to go through," or, "The space between the stuffed cats is bigger than it looks, it's just they're so furry you'd never know," or, "The plate curves so coins slide off except for the ones they glued on to look like winners."

"Astounding," Theo said.

"Carter, how would you like a pink flamingo?" Leila asked.

"To eat?" Carter joked. "Or as a pet?"

"Up to you!" she said, pointing to the flock of stuffed pink birds hanging from the ceiling of the Ring Toss booth.

Carter laughed, then said, "But we know it's rigged."

"Yeah, but beating a *rigged* game is more fun." Ridley smirked. "Win once, all you get is a tiny parrot. Win twice, you get a sketchy-looking bear. But win all three throws and you walk away with a giant pink flamingo. It's the biggest prize in the whole carnival. Everyone will notice how great we really are!"

Carter actually didn't *want* to be noticed.

"If you look around, you'll notice *no one* has a fla-mingo," Leila said. "No one wins the best prizes. But we're going to be the first."

Carter's face flushed. His instinct told him to turn and run away. Instead he forced himself to ask, "Why are you guys being so nice to me?"

Theo scrunched up his face, confused. "Why would we *not* be nice to you?"

Ridley crossed her arms and scowled. "It's so you can *belong*, dummy. We all know what it's like to feel the opposite."

Carter had to force a smile away to keep from look-ing like a fool.

Leila walked up to the booth runner and said, "Three tickets for three rings, please!" She handed one ring to Ridley, one to Theo, and kept one for herself.

"Ladies first," Theo said.

Ridley rolled over. Her eyes sized up the distance, the green bottles, the weight of the ring in her hand, and so on.

"Come on, we don't have all day," the booth run-ner said. Ridley tossed the ring, and it landed on the first bottle. She stuck her tongue out at the man.

Leila stepped up next. She stretched her arms over-head and cracked her knuckles. Standing on one leg, the other extended behind her, she bent forward, leaning as far over the rail as possible. She gave a slight toss and the ring landed on the closest bottle.

"That's cheating," the booth runner hissed.

"No, it's not," Leila said, still stretched out over the rail. "It says no touching the rail. I'm not touch-ing. I'm hovering above."

"Step back!" the booth runner insisted.

"Hey, buddy!" Ridley waved from her wheelchair, her red brows furrowed. "During my turn I couldn't even get close to the railing, so let's just call it even, whaddya say?"

The booth runner took a step back with a huff.

Then it was Theo's turn. He slid his violin bow out of his pants pocket. (This time, Carter saw the folding mechanism lock into place.) Theo waved the bow over the ring on the counter and it began to float. Carter held his breath. He still didn't know how Theo made things levitate.

The ring danced into the air. The booth runner looked like he was going to faint. A second later, the ring landed gently on one of the bottles with a satisfying clink!

"Yes!" Carter pumped his fist. He couldn't help it.

"One flamingo a-go-go, please!" said Leila.

Still scratching his head, the booth runner handed them the giant prize. The four friends high-fived and burst into laughter. Ridley rolled triumphantly down the midway as Leila skipped beside her, the giant pink flamingo bobbing atop her shoulders. On the other side of the wheelchair, Theo stepped along in his usual way. Carter weaved in front of them, unable to hide his excitement. "How did you do that?"

"A real magician never reveals her secrets," said Ridley.

"Oh, that old myth," Theo said with a chuckle.

"Not a myth," said Ridley. "It's a rule of real magic."

"You wouldn't know *real magic* if it bit you on the knee," Carter said.

Ridley gazed down to find the words REAL MAGIC on her pants leg. Carter had snuck the words off his shoe and onto her knee without her noticing. Ridley half smiled, impressed.

"You didn't let me finish," said Ridley. "I was *going* to say that a magician never reveals her secrets to *just anyone*. How'd I beat the ring toss? By gauging the weight and using simple physics."

"There's this thing called gravity," Leila said with a playful shrug. "You've probably heard of it: a very helpful law of nature. I used that. Since the rings are made of super-springy plastic, the closer you are, the less they bounce."

"And you?" Carter asked Theo. "Ready to finally tell me the secret of your bow?"

Theo considered, then said, "Not yet."

Everyone laughed.

TEN

After beating one of the unbeatable games, the four friends went to the fun house and the hall of mirrors. When the others went to the sideshow, Carter excused himself, saying he needed the bathroom. In actuality, he didn't want any of Bosso's gang to find him in there again.

Finally, they each tried their might at the Test Your Strength machine. None of them won. "It's the one game in the whole place that isn't rigged," Leila noted.

"Oh, it's rigged all right," Ridley groaned, "if you're not a giant hulk with huge muscles."

"We have to ride the Ferris wheel!" Leila cried, dragging the others along.

The four of them made their way into a rusty caged car. As the ground retreated beneath them, Carter's stomach dropped and he came face-to-face with the full moon. Ridley called out to the woman at the controls, "Keep an eye on my chair, please! That bell was very expensive!" When the others stared at her, aghast, she added, "What? You guys are the only ones allowed to crack jokes?"

The metal car jerked to a halt at the wheel's highest point and swung slightly in the wind. Leila rocked back and forth next to Carter, making the car swing harder.

"Cut it out," growled Ridley. "You're going to make me puke tiny cucumber and cream cheese sandwiches everywhere."

"Sorry!" Leila said. "It's this cage....I'm always thinking of an escape."

"You're going to rock your way out?" Ridley asked.

"Maybe!"

For a moment there was nothing but the wind and the squeaking of the swinging car. As Carter looked out over the small town, he felt that warm feeling wash over him. He was on top of the world in more ways than one.

"Do you guys like it here?" Carter asked.

"In Mineral Wells?" Ridley said. "Sure. As small towns go, it's not so bad."

"Not so bad?" Leila chimed in. "It's wonderful! There's fresh air. The trees and hills are great for hikes. The people are nice—"

"The people are *okay*," Ridley interrupted.

"I guess the kids at my school aren't so great," Leila admitted. "But I don't think they mean to be as cruel as they are."

Ridley nudged Theo's arm and then whispered to him, "Uh, *yes* they do." He smiled politely at her.

"You always think the best of everyone, don't you?" Carter asked. He'd never known someone like Leila.

"I try to," Leila said, her voice dropping. "Before I was adopted, I lived in an orphanage. It...wasn't wonderful. So ever since, I've tried to be thankful. It's not easy. But it's better than feeling sorry for myself."

DING-DING-DING-DING-DING.

(That was the sound of a bell from someone winning a prize down on the midway, but I bet you thought it was a symbol that Carter suddenly realized he and

Leila had lots in common. Nope! It was just a bell...)

(...Or *was* it?)

"I never feel sorry for myself," Ridley said. "Whenever I'm angry or frustrated or lonely, I put the energy into something constructive, like practicing magical transformations."

After the Ferris wheel, they regrouped in the center of the midway as crowds of people pushed around them. Theo checked his watch. "We have time for one more activity before the big-top show begins."

"Maybe your parents will be there, Carter," said Ridley. "*Everyone* loves a big-top show."

"Your *parents*?" Leila asked. "I thought—"

Flustered, Carter blurted out, "Oh! Well, I mentioned to Ridley that we're staying at the resort up the hill." He wiped sweat from his forehead. *Stupid*, he thought. *If they find out I lied, they'll never talk to me again.* "But none of that's important right now." He hated to flash Uncle Sly's smile at them, but he didn't know what else to do. "I think Theo's right! Let's get out of this horde and find somewhere else to go."

A purple tent with golden tassels was only steps away. Outside, a wooden sign said PSYCHIC. "Hurry," said Carter. "This way!" He held the velvet curtain aside for the others, then grabbed the coins he'd found in his pocket that morning. This wasn't an emergency, and it certainly wouldn't fill his belly, but he wanted to do something special for the others. They'd given him the best night of his life, and he wanted to give them something in return.

The walls of the dim tent were decorated with intricate indigo tapestries. Incense perfumed the air with a dark, spicy aroma. In the center was a round table draped in faded red scarves. A wrinkled old woman sat gazing at a cloudy crystal ball.

"The Gatekeepers of Destiny have brought you to Helga," she said, her eyes darting among their faces. "Your future waits to be revealed."

"Give me a break," muttered Ridley.

Carter set a coin on the table. Helga snatched it and tucked it inside her belt. "You must hold one another's hands." She arranged herself on her chair and waved her palms over the cloudy crystal ball.

"Bring forth the future and give me true sight," she chanted. "Unfurl their path in darkness or light. Show me the way these four will tread. Reveal what's to come...be it white, black, or red."

She brought her face close to the crystal ball. The

milky whiteness within the glass swirled and cleared, like clouds parting to reveal the sky.

Helga's eyes froze, transfixed. "I see..." She bent closer. "A new friendship has formed among you. One of you is a traveler. One of you has great advantage. Another has terrible hardships. And the last of you has much love to share. But each of you has a long road ahead. It will be hard at times, but if you work together and stay true to one another, nothing will bar you. Alone you are weak. Together you are strong. So say the Gatekeepers of Destiny."

As the friends exited, Leila said, "Did you hear

that? She knew everything about us! Mind blown!"

"No way," Ridley said. "All that was a bunch of generic mumbo jumbo. I've read fortune cookies with more insight."

"True or not, I liked her message," Theo said. "Sometimes it is worth a little pocket change to feel reassured."

"I liked it too," Carter agreed.

Sure, it was probably just the usual trickery of psychics, Carter thought, but what if she was right? What if the Gatekeepers of Destiny did want Carter to stay here?

Across the carnival, sirens blared and clowns ran around calling, "Time for the big show at the big top! One and all, come and join!"

"I think my...uh...my parents are probably waiting for me back at the resort," Carter mentioned, trying again to avoid being seen by Bosso's gang. "Maybe we should just go."

"But we already have tickets," said Theo.

"Don't be a goose, Carter," Leila said, doing a cart-wheel. "Madame Helga said it herself. Together, we're strong." She tilted her head as she examined his face quizzically, as if searching for the truth. "*Your parents won't mind*, I'm sure of it."

Reluctantly, Carter followed his friends.

The big show was in the largest tent at the center of the carnival. The Pock-Pickets were already on the circular stage, wearing their striped costumes, as Carter and the others made their way through the crowd and found their seats.

Theo tossed Carter a knowing look, reminding him of how they'd foiled the barbershop quartet's

pickpocketing plan that afternoon. It felt so long ago. Carter wondered if he should be ready to help stop them from stealing again.

They sang:

"We've had fun, we've had laughs.
You've played games—all those gaffes!
Cotton candy, popcorn too,
Corn dogs made of not-a-clue,
Rides that tossed you to and fro,
And now it's time for the big show!"

As they sang, the Pock-Pickets made a human arch, one pair of them standing on the shoulders of the other two and pressing their palms together.

"The night's caboose is the best part.
You fed the horse, now here's the cart,
The man who makes your dreams come true,
The Brilliant Boss of Ballyhoo,
The grand, the great, the Heavyweight,
Master of You-Never-Know:
It's the man of the hour, B. B. BOSSO!"

With a burst of flame and smoke, the Pock-Pickets vanished and were replaced by B. B. Bosso center stage. The large man with the white-powdered face wore a black silk robe that shimmered with shiny beads, and a wide and crooked smile. The angry blond monkey that Carter had seen the previous night was perched on his shoulder, wearing the same red fez.

"Greetings! I am B. B. Bosso and this is my show! All you see, you see because of me! All your fun is by my design! I've crisscrossed the globe to learn the mysteries of the mystics, the secrets of the swamis, the fabulosities of the fakirs. Why? It thrills me beyond all measure to entertain you, my beloved fans!"

The crowd clapped and laughed. Carter ducked a little lower among the others and tucked his hat down. He hoped his friends didn't notice his behavior.

Bosso started the show with a *SWISH* by swinging a sword and chopping the heads off a bouquet of roses— dandelions popped up in their place. "Not bad," Ridley said as the crowd oohed and aahed.

Then Bosso swung up his clenched fists and levitated a donkey fifteen feet above the stage. It thrashed its legs in the air, desperate to get away. "That poor animal," Leila whispered as the crowd gasped.

For the next trick, a frightened-looking clown stumbled onto the stage, as though pushed from the wings. Bosso shut him inside a coffin-like box laid out on a table. The clown squeezed his eyes shut when Bosso held up a handsaw, its teeth as big as a shark's. Bosso sawed the clown's box into threes. First he cut at the knees, then at the neck. Bosso's brow was shiny with sweat from the effort. Carter was flustered, worried that something might go terribly wrong. But after a few toe-curling moments, Bosso put the clown back together again. The clown staggered off stage in a daze.

Two cannons fired, shooting clowns across the stage into nets. Then Bosso flung doves into the air, which changed instantly into black crows, cawing loudly overhead like a bad omen.

"He has an interesting technique," Theo said, his eyes fixed on the stage.

"You might wonder what it takes to run a carnival." Bosso grinned. "Let me tell you.

"It takes *strength*!" He juggled four sledgehammers, then stepped away from them. They kept circling in the air.

"It takes *money*!" A giant safe was rolled on stage by the Tattooed Baby. B. B. Bosso spun it around, showing all four sides. When he opened it, a great explosion of bills rained over the crowd. The bills weren't money, though—they were blank pieces of green paper.

"It takes *flair!*" From the sides of the stage, the Walrus tossed several white chairs to B. B. Bosso, who threw them together to create a tower, each new chair balanced atop the last. The Spider-Lady climbed up the side and crouched on top.

"It takes *power!*" With a snap of B. B. Bosso's fingers, the tower collapsed. The Spider-Lady didn't move. Instead she and the top chair floated in place.

Carter wasn't sure but he thought that she might have smiled right at him. He slunk down even lower in his seat.

"It takes *laughs!*" B. B. Bosso returned to the safe, closed it, and opened it again. In place of the money, one Pock-Picket after another climbed out, waving to the crowd.

"It takes *magic!*" B. B. Bosso raised his arms and all of his lackeys—the Walrus, the Tattooed Baby, and the Spider-Lady—floated to the center of the stage. "And most important, it takes *ALL OF YOU!*"

Curtains fell around the stage from rafters overhead. A moment later they dropped to the ground, revealing giant mirrors surrounding the stage and reflecting the image of the crowd back at themselves. The mirrors appeared on the stage so quickly that people shouted in awe.

A spotlight swiveled toward center stage, and the mirrors became transparent, revealing Bosso with his monkey sitting on his shoulder. Everyone else who'd been with them had disappeared. The crowd went wild.

Bosso's monkey clapped its tiny hands as the rest of Bosso's crew rejoined him center stage. Finally, all of them took a bow.

"Thank you, one and all!" Bosso blared. "One last thing. As many of you know, the largest diamond in the world, the Star of Africa, will be traveling through this very town. I have arranged that it—all five hundred and thirty carats—will be part of a very special show, the Finale Fantastic. Tomorrow night at the Grand Oak Resort! Please come, invite your friends, and be prepared for my most amazing feat yet! Good night, and thank you!"

The spotlight flickered out for a brief moment and then came up fully again. But Bosso and his gang had vanished from the stage.

HOW TO...

Make a Color Prediction!

Hello again! I didn't expect you back so soon. Someone is certainly a fast reader. Good for you. You want to learn more magic, eh? Brilliant. Pull up a seat. Oh, I see. You're already sitting. Well, let's go, then.

A big part of being a magician is performing in front of an audience. There isn't anything quite like the feeling you get while amazing your friends and family (and pets!) with tricks you've practiced, practiced, and practiced some more. Seeing those faces light up with thrill and delight is worth all that hard work. (Plus, you might be able to get out of doing chores.)

Thus, I thought you might enjoy a trick you can do for a crowd. Small kids love this one! It is perfect for younger siblings, cousins, or anyone who might have crayons lying around. Time to learn how to PREDICT A CRAYON'S COLOR BASED ON ITS WEIGHT!

WHAT YOU NEED:

A box of crayons
An audience

HELPFUL HINTS (PRACTICE!):

I highly recommend practicing this with a friend. Once you can pull it off with them, you can do better with a big audience.
Remember: Practice, practice, practice! (Then nap. Then snack. Then...You know the drill....Let's all say it together: KEEEEEP PRAAAAAACTICING!!!!!! Very good, you clever creatures!)

STEPS:

1. Give a member of the audience a box of crayons. (You can also ask someone to bring crayons.)

2. Turn your back to the audience, placing your hand behind you.

3. Ask one audience member to pick a single crayon and place it in the palm of your hand.

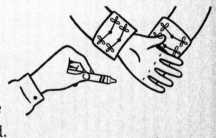

4. This is a good time for you to say something like "Did you know every color has its own special weight? Only a practiced magician can tell the difference. For instance, green is heavier than yellow. Red is heavier than blue, and black is surprisingly light!" Of course, you can make up your own speech. The key is to keep your audience entertained.

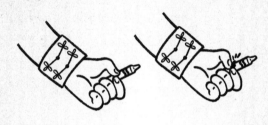

**Secret magician movement: While you are talking, scratch a little off the crayon tip with your fingernail.

5. While you are still standing with your back to the audience, say something like "Okay, I've got it. I don't want you to think I'm peeking, so take the crayon and put it back into the box."

6. Now turn to face your audience members.

**Second secret magician movement: While turning, sneak a peek at the fingernail that scratched the crayon. You will see what color it was by the part you scratched off!*

7. Announce the color of the crayon to your audience. They will be amazed and delighted!

8. Don't forget to take a bow.

ELEVEN

When the show ended, Carter felt relief wash over him. He and his friends were unharmed and intact.

Throngs of people walked along the main road back to the warm lights of their homes. It seemed half of Mineral Wells had attended tonight's show. But Carter was only concerned with three of them. Oblivious to his anxieties, Leila told jokes to Carter. He almost interrupted her several times to ask about her life in the orphanage. He wanted to tell her the truth about his own history. Instead he laughed. Ridley and Theo trailed behind, discussing the likely mechanisms behind Bosso's show.

They were almost back to the magic shop when Theo turned pale. He stopped walking. "My bow is gone."

He patted his pant leg again and again. Then he checked his jacket, as though it might have ended up in there. It was nowhere to be found.

"My lucky lockpicks!" Leila said, her face dropping. "I always have them in my front pocket. But they've vanished!"

Ridley checked a hidden compartment in the arm of her wheelchair. "Leila, please tell me this is a joke. I *need* my notebook. My whole life is in there."

"I'm sorry." Leila's voice cracked. "I'd never make a joke like this."

Carter's heart raced. He had only one thing of true value. He opened his satchel and dug deep. The small wooden box was gone. In its place was a torn piece of paper.

When Carter looked up, Theo, Leila, and Ridley also had torn pieces of paper in their hands. They put the four pieces together to form a note. It read:

You shouldn't have messed with the Pock-Pickets.

P.S. Carter, you should have joined Bosso, not those misfits!

"What do they mean by 'joined Bosso'?" Ridley asked, her eyes stabbing at Carter.

Carter felt like someone had just pushed him off a cliff. "Last night...he asked me to join his gang," he admitted quickly and quietly.

"Did you?" Theo asked.

"Of course not!"

"How can we trust a word he says?" Ridley growled.

"Now, hold on," Leila said. "If Carter was with them, he wouldn't have been robbed too."

"For all we know, this is part of his shtick," Ridley said. "He gets all friendly, robs us blind, and then pretends he got robbed too."

"I don't steal!" Carter shouted.

"Yeah, right!" Ridley yelled back. "And I just ride around in this chair for the fun of it!"

Leila and Theo stepped in between Carter and Ridley. "That's enough," the violinist said calmly.

"Remember what the psychic lady said? We all have to work together," Leila added.

"That was a bunch of hooey," Ridley spat. "And it was Carter's idea to see the old lady. Maybe that's part of the whole deal."

"What whole deal?" Carter defended himself. "I'm... I'm not lying." Not at the moment, he thought, cringing at what he'd told them about staying at the resort on the hill. He found that he could barely look at Leila.

"That's probably a lie too," Ridley went on. "I'm going back for my journal."

"That's a terrible idea," Carter said. "Bosso has a whole army of goons. You don't stand a chance by yourself."

"Then we'll all go," Leila said.

"Four against an entire carnival?" Theo said. "I think perhaps we need to contact the police and explain our situation."

"NO!" Carter yelped. "Please, no cops."

"See?" Ridley said. "He is a thief!"

"I am not! I'm...I'm a runaway."

The night became suddenly quiet. Leila, Theo, and Ridley stared at Carter. Despite the darkness, he felt like a giant spotlight was on him.

"You don't have a home?" Leila asked softly.

"No," Carter admitted. "I have an uncle, but he isn't a good person. He wanted me to steal from people, but I wouldn't. So I ran away. I hopped a train and ended up here. I'm not a thief. But if you call the

cops, I'll go away to foster care or worse." He checked Leila's face for reassurance. But her eyes were blank. She looked like she was lost in memory. "They'll take me away from Mineral Wells, and I'll never see any of you again. And I would hate that, more than anything. I would never steal from any of you. I would never hurt you. You're...you're the first friends I've ever had. You have to believe me."

There was a long period of silence. Carter felt his heart sink further and further. His three new friends were going to walk away, and he would be alone again.

Then something unexpected happened.

"I believe you," said Leila. She hugged Carter.

"So do I," said Theo. He patted Carter on the back.

"Well, I don't...." Ridley said, her arms crossed. "But I'm willing to think about it."

"No one should be in foster care, or live in an orphanage. Everyone desrves a home," Leila said sadly. She took a deep breath, then added, "But you hopped a train? So neato!"

"I cannot imagine what you've been through," Theo said. "My condolences. I'm sorry you didn't tell us sooner. But I understand why you hesitated."

"I'm not sorry," Ridley said, arms still crossed. "But

it sounds like your life sucks. I can relate." She knocked her fist on the arm of her wheelchair. "Truce?"

"Truce." Carter beamed. He'd never felt such relief. He took a deep breath, his whole body shuddering—it felt like the first oxygen he'd ever inhaled. "But what do we do now? We have to get our stuff back."

"We do," Theo said. "But it's late, we're tired, and we're four kids against an entire carnival of crooks. Cooler heads will prevail in the morning. I find one always works best after a good night's sleep, a shower, and a well-rounded breakfast."

"That's not how I would have put it, but fine," Ridley said. "First thing in the morning."

"Agreed," Leila chirped. "Since tomorrow's Saturday, let's meet at ten at the magic shop?"

Everyone nodded.

Ridley and Leila said good night, then went on their way. Carter was about to head back to the park when Theo asked, "Do you have a place to sleep?"

"I can take care of myself," Carter said. He sounded tougher than he felt.

"Unacceptable." Theo shook his head. "You are staying with me."

TWELVE

Carter woke to the sound of music. A violin, he guessed, once he remembered where he was. He was stretched out in a bed with a real mattress, cotton sheets, a knitted blanket, and two pillows. His feet didn't even stick out at the end of the covers, like they did with the newspapers that he and Uncle Sly had sometimes used for bedding.

Sunlight glowed through the gauzy curtain. A gentle breeze fluttered in.

This must be what heaven is like, Carter thought. A brief image flickered in his mind: a tiny bedroom in that red cottage with the white trim, morning sunlight streaming in, the sound of his parents' voices rising from the kitchen below. There was more...so much more...he wished he could remember.

It was a very clean guest room. There was a full-size bed, a small shelf with fresh flowers in a vase, and an easel in the corner. The previous evening, Theo had mentioned that his mother was a painter. The walls were hung with pages clipped from magazines, sketches, postcards, and photos of several stained-glass windows.

Carter stood and stretched. He hadn't worn pajamas in a long time—not since before he'd ended up with Uncle Sly. These were *very* comfy. A strange noise echoed up from the backyard. Peering out the window, Carter noticed what looked like a large wooden shed, its walls made of wire mesh. White feathers were scattered in the grass like a halo surrounding it.

"Breakfast!" called a woman's singsong voice. This had to be Theo's mother.

Carter crept to the door and pressed his ear against it.

Downstairs, the violin breathed out its final hopeful note. There was light clapping, followed by a resonant voice saying, "That was beautiful, son."

"Thank you, Father. I'll go see if my guest is ready to eat." Footfalls ran up the stairs, followed by a soft knock on the door. "May I come in?"

"Of course—it's your house," Carter said. When Theo walked in, Carter asked, "Do you ever *not* wear a tuxedo?"

"Not unless I'm wearing pajamas," Theo answered. "Anyway, just a reminder of last night when we got in: We told my parents you're a prospective student at Mineral Wells Academy and that the dean asked us to care for you during your visit."

"I remember," Carter reassured him. They'd decided to keep what happened with the Pock-Pickets a secret. Theo's parents would only have wanted to alert the authorities. "I'll be fine. I've been in a lot tighter jams than this."

"I have to go out and feed the doves, but feel free to head downstairs whenever you're ready."

"So those are doves in the pen out back?"

"They make for very interesting pets." Theo gave his signature nod. "See you soon!"

There was a spare set of slippers for him to wear. The bathroom soaps were shaped like seashells. After Carter took a nice, long, warm shower (the best of his life), he headed downstairs. In the hall, the sky-blue walls were decorated with Italian opera posters in white frames. There were other frames too: pictures of a very young Theo surrounded by four other kids who looked almost exactly like him. Siblings! *Funny*, Carter thought. *Theo hadn't mentioned any of them.* Academic awards and diplomas were mixed in with the artwork, each one containing a different name. They must have belonged to Theo's older brothers and sisters.

When Carter padded down the stairs, he saw a trumpet hanging over the fireplace and a lamp-crowned tower of books stacked neatly beside the leather sofa. Best of all, everything smelled clean. After years on the streets and in halfway houses, Carter wasn't used to things that smelled nice.

"Have a seat, Carter," Theo's mother offered gently. She placed a soft-boiled egg before him, in a little ceramic cup adorned with flowers that she had decorated herself. It was accompanied by a tiny silver spoon. "Did you sleep okay?" She was tall and her features were delicate. Carter could see where Theo had gotten his regal profile. She was dressed in a crisp white blouse and soft denim pants that were spattered with colorful paint. She wore her hair pulled back, tucked under a folded green paisley bandanna.

"It was the best sleep I think I've ever had," Carter said truthfully.

"I am so pleased to hear that. With all my oldest children out of the house, it's nice to know that their rooms can be of use."

When he went to dip into the egg with his spoon, Carter realized that it had turned into a golf ball. Theo grinned mischievously.

"Theo," chided his mother, "no magic at the table."

"You sound like Mr. Vernon," Theo noted before returning Carter's egg.

"My son tells me you will be staying in Mineral Wells for some time," Theo's father said. He had kind eyes and his black hair was flecked with gray.

"That's the plan."

"Well...I hope you like it here."

"I already do!"

"Mineral Wells Academy is top-notch. Excellent music program. What instrument do you play?" Theo's father asked.

"Not everybody plays an instrument," Theo said. He turned to Carter. "My dad conducts the local symphony. He wishes the world was more musical than it is."

"Ah, son, that's where you're wrong," Theo's father said. "The world is filled with more music than most people notice." He patted Carter's hand. "Pick up an instrument. You won't regret it."

On their way to Vernon's Magic Shop, Carter said, "You know, I should be worried. But what you said last night is totally true. After a good night's sleep, a warm shower, and a square meal, I feel on top of the world—like I could tackle anything, even Bosso."

"Well, I'm glad you feel good," Theo said, "but let's hope it doesn't come to that."

The boys kept their eyes peeled in case any of Bosso's goons were prowling the streets. But as they turned onto Main Street, they found themselves stuck in a swarm of shoppers and sightseers. "Who are all these people?" Carter asked.

"Tourists," Theo explained. "Warm weekends always attract the largest crowds. They stay at the resort and come down during the day to go shopping."

"Great," Carter said. "They're a bunch of sitting ducks. Bosso and his crooked carnies are going to go on a stealing spree tonight."

"You really don't like Bosso, do you?" Theo asked.

"He reminds me of my uncle, only times a thousand. My uncle stole to eat. But Bosso just steals because he's greedy. We have to stop him and his goons." At that moment, something tickled the back of Carter's brain, like he was trying to remember something about Bosso's clowns.

Theo interrupted, distracting Carter. "Perhaps we should just focus on getting our own stuff back first. Once we have that, we'll have proof to notify the authorities without getting you into trouble. Then we can help other victims safely."

As the pair walked through Mineral Wells, Carter

observed more of the quaint town. Of all the places he had been, Mineral Wells was uniquely beautiful. The firehouse's red engines gleamed in the open garage. The barbershop had a red-and-white-striped pole and friendly barbers who waved at passersby. The men and women working the counter at the ice-cream parlor wore flimsy paper hats and made giant sundaes. And everyone in town had a smile on their face. It was perfection.

When the boys walked into Mr. Vernon's shop, the parrot cried, "Meow. Meow. I'm a cat."

"That bird is hilarious," Carter said.

"Is she?" Mr. Vernon asked with a kind smile. He appeared suddenly from behind the counter. Today he wore another sharp black suit. "Well, she's certainly smart. Most yellow-naped Amazon parrots are highly intelligent animals. They have the uncanny ability to mimic human speech and cadence. Perfect as door greeters. They can also deliver secret messages if properly trained."

"Is Leila awake, sir?" Theo asked politely.

"I'm more than merely *awake*," Leila said from above.

When Carter and Theo looked up, they found Leila wrapped in chains and padlocks and hanging upside down from the nearly twenty-foot ceiling. "Someone start the stopwatch," she said.

Mr. Vernon held up his pocket watch. With a click, he said, "You may start."

Leila began shaking and shivering and moving.

"Is that safe?" Carter asked.

"An excellent question," Mr. Vernon said. "Usually I would say no, but Leila is quite skilled. Though I suppose as her father, I should make her wear a helmet." He pulled a small notebook from his jacket and jotted down the word *helmet* before tucking it away.

The tiny bell on the door jingled as Ridley wheeled in.

"Hello, hello. How are you today?" Presto the Parrot asked.

"Hey, Presto." Ridley reached up and scratched the parrot's yellow neck. "Morning, Mr. V."

"Good morning to you as well, Ms. Larsen. Thirty seconds, Leila."

"I'm trying to get my time under a minute," Leila said, struggling. One chain and the lock fell free. "But it's hard without my lucky lockpicks."

"You lost your lucky lockpicks?" Vernon asked.

"She didn't lose them," Theo answered. "They were stolen."

"By Bosso's goons, last night at the carnival," Ridley added.

"I didn't want to worry you, Dad," Leila went on.

"Are you sure it was them?" Vernon asked.

"Positive," Theo said. He put the Pock-Pickets' note on the counter for Vernon to read. "They robbed each of us of a prized item and left us a note."

"They called you misfits? Well, that's rude," Mr. Vernon said. "And stealing is a filthy habit—like chewing gum."

"I think stealing is worse than chewing gum, Dad," Leila said. Another chain and padlock slunk off and hit the floor. She still had one more chain and padlock.

"Sixty seconds, sweetie," Vernon said to Leila.

"Aww, pickles," she moaned.

"Well, I'm sorry to hear that the carnival workers stole your things. But *things* can be replaced."

"They weren't carnies," said Ridley. "They were a barbershop quartet."

"Even worse," Mr. Vernon cried out.

"Actually, they took something from me that can't be replaced," Carter said. "It's one of a kind, really. And it means a lot to me."

"My bow didn't hold true sentimental value, but

I would like it back," Theo said. "It's hard to make things levitate without it."

"And my journal has months of great ideas in it." Ridley flexed her fists. "I'd rather bust some skulls than start over."

"Well, I don't think it should come to fisticuffs," Mr. Vernon said. "Perhaps there's a more subtle solution?"

"We know they're staying at the Grand Oak Resort," Leila said, swinging around like a fish caught on a line. "If we find what room they're in, perhaps we could sneak in and get our stuff back, and no one would be any wiser?"

"That's not a half-bad idea," Mr. Vernon said. "If a small group were to sneak in, it might be better to have two teams. One keeping an eye on the villains, and another to make the grab. Hypothetically speaking, of course. I don't condone such behavior at all." Vernon gave Carter a wink.

The last padlock unlocked and the final chain fell to the floor. Leila reached up, uncuffed her ankles, and then flipped to the floor like a graceful acrobat. "What was my final time?"

"One minute, forty-two seconds," Mr. Vernon said. "Quite good for losing your lucky lockpicks."

"But not great," Leila said. "I need them back."

"You know, I recall the Other Mr. Vernon mentioning that he had to feed those 'insufferable clowns' again at lunchtime. That might be an opportune moment to search their rooms," Mr. Vernon said. "I suppose, if you accidentally wandered into the wrong room, it would be an *accident* and not *illegal*. Something to keep in mind, in case..."

"Mr. Vernon, are you suggesting that we—" Theo started.

Mr. Vernon quickly cut him off. "Absolutely not! I would never! Only a group of absolute *misfits* would think up such an outrageous scheme." He crossed the room and knocked a box off the shelf. Several wigs, hats, and glasses fell out. "Oops. I'm such a klutz. Leila, would you and your friends mind picking these up? Feel free to borrow any of them if you like. I often find changing one's look to be an advantage in awkward situations."

Carter, Leila, Theo, and Ridley—the misfits that they were—looked at one another with mischievous smiles.

THIRTEEN

You'll notice this book has no thirteenth chapter. As you probably already know, thirteen is a very unlucky number. While I don't believe in luck, I do believe in magic. And (as I have mentioned before) magic comes in all shapes and sizes. And occasionally, it comes in the form of bad magic, such as tripping over your feet, falling down stairs, or making a poor grade on an important test because you genuinely forgot to study. Okay...I suppose I do believe in bad luck.

But that's beside the point. As most buildings do not have a thirteenth floor, I am choosing not to have a thirteenth chapter. Instead, I'm going to allow you to use this time to take a much-needed bathroom break. Go on, then. I'll wait.

...

Done already? That was quick.

I hope you washed your hands because you're about to use them to turn pages faster than ever!

FOURTEEN

Nearly an hour later, the four misfits made their way up Grand Oak Drive, and Carter found himself nearly stumbling in awe. The sides of the cobblestone road were adorned with sculptures, fountains, and shrubs shaped like zoo animals. It was another warm and sunny day. As he stepped beneath a leafy green giraffe, he said, "I've never been anywhere like this."

In the daylight, the cluster of buildings at the top of the hill gleamed white. At the center of all of them stood an ample three-story lodge. Each floor was marked by thirteen expansive windows. Leila mentioned that this was the building where most of the guests stayed. It was all gables and turrets and green-and-white-striped awnings. Half a dozen chimneys rose from the jagged roof, and in the middle of them all sat a small cupola, a simple weather vane perched on top, swaying in the soft breeze. The road led up the slope to a covered turnaround with a grand entryway directly in its middle. Beyond the wide front doors were hidden a massive restaurant and an even larger theater.

The other buildings were smaller. Wide white signs with black lettering were posted on the walls just outside their front doors. ATHLETICS ROOM. DANCE STUDIO. CLIMBING COURSE. READING ROOM. ROPE COURSE. TEA ROOM. MINERAL SPA. JUICE BAR. And many more. All were connected by labyrinthine stone paths, stretches of which were covered by wisteria canopies. Dark slate overlaid the peaks and gables of the dramatic rooflines, and green shutters accented every window.

The Grand Oak Resort was magnificent.

If you wanted to try horseback riding, you could. How about ballroom dancing? They'd teach you. If anyone wished for a mud bath that might make them look ten years younger...well, that could be done too. How about a buffet with all-you-can-eat seven-layer chocolate cake? They had it...*for breakfast*! But many agreed the best part was the show on the stage in the main building each night after dinner. During the weekdays, the Grand Oak staff and the guests would show off their talents. Singing. Juggling. Dancing. However, on the weekends, big acts—some of the greatest crooners, comedians, musicians, and, yes, magicians of the age—took the stage.

"So luxurious," Leila said as she led the group past the last of the topiary animals. "Since Poppa cooks here, I get to come hang out in the kitchen sometimes. So I know this place like the back of my hand. After hours, I find empty rooms to practice my escape tricks in. There's even a whole wing that's been abandoned! And a garden maze around back near the woods where people are constantly getting lost and needing to be rescued."

Carter gazed up at the main hall's giant columns as Leila waved to a bellhop. The old man opened the monumental door for them with a strained smile. Leila said, "Thanks, Dean!" Carter was paralyzed by the grandeur, so Leila took his hand and tugged him inside.

The lobby was in full swing, with people of every shape, size, color, and age coming and going. Tourists

were at the concierge's desk asking about hiking trips and shopping for secondhand furniture and antique knickknacks. In fact, much of the decor in Vernon's Magic Shop came from little farms and houses all around Mineral Wells. People are always throwing away things that they think are junk but other people believe to be treasure.

The elevator doors opened and closed, taking in and pushing out families in need of nourishment or activity. Teenagers in dripping bathing suits zipped up and down the wooden staircase from the indoor pool to the dining hall.

A heaping brass luggage cart glided past, with a kid in an eye patch riding atop the highest suitcase, shouting commands like a pirate. Standing nine feet tall at the top of a staircase was a stuffed grizzly bear on its hind legs. Its claws were raised, but any fear factor was lost due to its sunglasses.

In the center of the room, a boy and a girl in matching plaid jumpsuits were tap-dancing on a small mirrored stage. An audience of guests gathered around to watch. Carter guessed the dancers were twins, but he wasn't sure if it was the matching outfits, hair color, and facial features, or the easy and perfectly in sync moves of their routine. Despite the dizzying speed of their clicking toes and their swinging arms, they never missed a beat.

When the song ended, they launched straight into the next part of their act. "Hey, Izzy, what do you call a troupe of tap-dancing chorizos?" the boy asked.

"I don't know, Olly," the girl answered. "What?"

"Tapas!" Olly's shoes did a *tappity-tap-tap-tap*.

"That's Olly and Izzy Golden," Leila said to Carter as she gave a wave. "They're great. Their parents work here at the resort too. Their dad teaches comedy

THE MAGIC MISFITS

techniques and their mom is a ballroom dance instructor. We may be good at magic, but those two kids know how to make people laugh."

"The first time I saw their show, I laughed so hard I cried," Ridley added. "And I never cry."

"I wonder if anyone has ever cried so hard they laughed," Theo mused.

"I could help you find out," Ridley said, tapping her fingers on the arm of her chair.

"Oh har-har-har."

"*I'm* gonna cry if I don't get my lucky lockpicks back," Leila said. Carter's heart began to race as he thought of what the Pock-Pickets might be doing to his wooden box. "Let's get going!" Leila led the others to the concierge—a stunning woman in a smart pantsuit with a silver name tag that said QUINN. "Hey, Q!" Leila said, giving her a hug. "How's life?"

"Wonderful!" Quinn said. "This weekend's been so much fun. The Grand Oak is sold out, and everyone is buzzing about Bosso's big show tonight. We don't know what he's going to do with that diamond. Maybe he'll make it even bigger!"

"I'd just *love* to get his autograph," Leila said

sarcastically, trying hard not to roll her eyes. "Poppa said he was cooking lunch for them today. Do you know what time and where?"

"Of course I do," the concierge said. "That's my job! Mr. Bosso and his guests will be lunching in the Commodore Room at one. But you can catch him before that—he and his friends are relaxing by the indoor pool." She leaned forward and whispered, "Maybe don't tell them I mentioned it. They've been a bit intense as of late."

"No problem, Q. You're a doll," Leila said. Leila led the others to a corner of the lobby. "So what's our plan?"

"Get dressed up," Ridley said, tapping the duffel bag resting in her lap, which was full of Mr. Vernon's props. "Then divide and conquer."

"Perfect," Carter said. "Let's get our stuff back."

"I don't want to come out," Carter said from the bathroom door. "Are you sure we don't have another disguise?"

"I only brought the four," Leila said. "One for each of us."

"Hurry it up," Ridley said. "We need to get going while the villains are making waves."

Carter stumbled from the bathroom into a hallway off the lobby. "I feel ridiculous."

Leila and Ridley burst out laughing. "You said you didn't want to be recognized," Theo noted with a grin. "I believe this will do the trick."

Carter had traded in his pants and shirt for a green Speedo, green goggles, and a green bathing cap.

The others were already dressed. Theo wore a bell-hop uniform, and Ridley was dressed as an old woman (complete with white wig and face makeup). Leila wore a one-piece swimsuit covered in sunflowers and a swim cap with little fabric flowers and beaded pearls.

"Want to trade?" Carter asked Theo. Theo shook his head.

"If you're that uncomfortable, *I'll* trade you." Leila giggled.

"Let's just get this done," Carter said.

When they got to the indoor pool, they all did some exploring.

The four friends took turns walking into the glass atrium at different times. Theo went first, pretending to work. Next, Ridley entered, pretending to look for a suitable space below the sunroof. Leila ran in and dove straight into the water. When Carter walked in, he froze. He'd never seen such an amazing place.

Despite the temperate spring weather outside, the glass atrium was warm as the sun came in from above and heated his skin. The air was scented with thrice-cooked french fries, suntan lotion, and chlorine. And the only sounds Carter heard were of splashes and laughter.

Shaped like a tropical lagoon, the pool had three levels of diving boards, a twisting slide, a rope swing, waterfalls, and a hot tub (for grown-ups only after five p.m.). Waiters in white shirts and pants hurried around with frozen lemonades and nachos, weaving among the lounge chairs surrounding the pool. It was like a splashy paradise.

Carter was in such awe, he didn't realize he was blocking the entrance. A large man called out directly behind him, "Hey, you…"

Fear rushed through Carter. It was Bosso.

FIFTEEN

Bosso towered over Carter. Today, Bosso was wearing a white tank top, black-and-white-striped swimming trunks, and rubber flip-flops that looked two sizes too small for his giant, hairy feet. Bosso and Carter stared at each other for a tense couple of seconds as Carter waited to be recognized. He expected Bosso to do something terrible.

Instead the carnival owner growled, "Move it, kid. You're in the doorway." Without waiting, he shoved past Carter.

"He didn't recognize me," Carter whispered to

himself. Leila's disguise worked. Bosso had no idea who he was.

Carter ran at the pool and formed himself into a cannonball. After coming up from the huge splash, he met Leila in the middle of the water. Together, they swam over toward the edge of the water where Bosso and his crew were camped. Like little frogs, the pair broke the surface and peered above the waterline with goggled eyes.

Bosso and his minions hogged the sun chair area around the deep end near the bar. Bosso was at the center, lying on his back, his eyes closed as two frown clowns in full makeup fanned him. The white from their faces was running in sweaty rivulets down their necks. The emerald ring on Bosso's finger flashed, and his hand held a white blended drink with an umbrella in it. Beside him, a thin woman in a black full-piece bathing suit took in the sun. It took Carter a moment to recognize the Spider-Lady without her extra arms. The Walrus stood directly behind them, eating chicken wings and tossing the bones right onto the tiled floor.

Half a dozen clowns of different sizes lounged in normal swimwear fashion from the neck down and in that same clown makeup from the neck up.

"Hey, look," Carter whispered to Leila. A man in a police uniform walked over to Bosso.

"That's Sheriff Shaw," Leila said. "What's he doing?"

Bosso handed him an envelope. The sheriff opened it and thumbed through a stack of money. He slipped the envelope into his sheriff's jacket.

"Looks like that cop is crooked," Carter said. "He's on Bosso's payroll? That can't be—"

Before he could say "good," Leila pulled him below the surface. The clowns had been staring at them quizzically. Her underwater hand gestures signaled that they should meet the others. Together, Leila and Carter swam to the shallow end near the palm trees. They hopped out of the pool and met Theo and Ridley behind the towel cabana. The four huddled together.

"His whole crew is here," Theo whispered, "except for the Pock-Pickets."

"The Tattooed Baby is missing too," Carter said.

"No, he's here," Ridley noted. "He's over at the poolside bar chomping on a cigar and hitting on ladies."

"Good for him," Leila said.

"Okay, we have half an hour until lunch," Ridley said, pointing to her watch. "Carter, Leila, you find a way into their room. Theo and I will stay here and keep a lookout. If they try to make a move, we'll slow them down."

"Oooh, I like that plan," said a scratchy-sounding voice.

"Me too," added a high-pitched voice. "But what do *we* do?"

Carter and Theo nearly fell over when they discovered Olly and Izzy standing directly behind them. "Where did you two come from?" Carter asked.

"We saw a team huddle," Olly said.

"We love team huddles," Izzy added. "But we're still unclear on the big-picture plan."

"You really want to help?" Leila asked.

"Leila!" Ridley hissed. "We already have one new kid. We can't have two more!"

"The more the merrier, I *always* say," Izzy said.

"You *never* say that," Olly quipped. "But we can help. We're good at distracting people."

"A mesmerizing distraction would be helpful...." Theo said.

"You don't even know what you'll be distracting Bosso and his gang from," Carter said to the twins.

"Even better," Izzy said. "Now, if you four get in

trouble, we can say we have no idea what's going on."

"That won't be hard for her," Olly said. "Izzy rarely knows what's going on."

"How are you going to distract them?" Carter asked.

The twins exchanged a mischievous smile. Then they ran over to the diving boards. They kicked off their shoes and climbed to the top of the high dive in their tap-dance outfits. When they got to the top, they yanked off their matching plaid jumpsuits to reveal a pair of matching plaid bodysuits. They stepped to the tip of the high diving board and said, "Hey, folks! Is

everyone having a good time?!" Since the acoustics in the room were very loud, their voices bounced all over, and everyone turned to look at them.

Clapping, cheers, and whistles ran through the pool crowd below.

"We don't know if you've heard, but we have a star in our midst!" Olly said.

"A star? You mean like the sun?" Izzy asked.

"No, silly. Someone much brighter: the master of carnival-ism, B. B. Bosso! Let's give him a round of applause." The crowd went wild, then Olly continued. "Bosso, any chance you'll take my sister next time you hit the road?"

"Watch it, or I'll hit you," Izzy said, winding up her arm comically. "But seriously, Mr. Bosso, you work hard to entertain. So for the next fifteen minutes, put your feet up, kick back, and let *us* repay the favor."

Bosso sat up in his chair and scowled, then glanced around to see everyone staring at him. He quickly smiled his famous crooked fake smile.

Olly gave the misfits a wink, and Leila said, "That's our cue. We have fifteen minutes."

"Theo and I will stay here," Ridley said. She handed

Leila her backpack. "If the wonder twins can't keep Bosso or his goons here, we'll buy you some time. But no matter what, you better hurry."

"How do you know where Bosso is staying?" Carter asked Leila during the elevator ride.

"When you were changing back into your regular clothes, I talked to the front desk. Perks of having a poppa who makes the best lobster risotto this side of the Rocky Mountains," Leila said. "Bosso and the Sideshowers are in the penthouse suite, and the rest of his goons are on the same floor."

"Bosso likes to be in control of everything," Carter said. He remembered the scene of the clowns and the tiny red car in the train yard from a couple nights prior. "My guess is he'll want to keep the important stuff in his room."

"Then I'll lead the way," Leila said. When the elevator doors opened, Leila and Carter peeked into the hallway. The four Pock-Pickets were humming a tune as they guarded Bosso's door.

"Aww, pickles," Leila whispered.

"What now?" Carter asked. The clock was ticking.

"Easy peasy," Leila said. "Follow me."

The pair went down one floor, ran into another hallway, and went through a door marked SERVICE ELE-VATOR.

"This leads to a back door on the top floor," Leila said, cracking her knuckles.

"Good thing you know this hotel so well," Carter remarked.

"A worthy escape artist should know where all exits are at all times. Something I learned back at the orphanage." Leila grinned.

"Maybe...maybe sometime when we're not pilfer-ing our stolen stuff back, you can tell me what that was like. The orphanage, I mean. We might have a lot in common."

To his surprise, Leila's face went blank. "Yeah, maybe," she said before stepping toward the elevator door.

Carter felt his own cheeks burn. Bringing up the orphanage might have been a mistake.

When they got out of the service elevator, Leila tried the handle: locked. She pulled a small gum-stick-size box from her swim cap. In it were little oddly shaped metal picks. Leila poked them into the service door lock, and a moment later it *click*ed. The door cracked open. "These aren't my lucky picks, but I always have a spare set. After all, a good escape artist needs to know how to open any door at any time."

"Are you sure you've never been a thief?" asked Carter.

"Maybe in a past life," she said coolly.

Warily, they entered the penthouse suite. The walls were paneled with extravagant walnut wood. Landscape paintings hung in gold frames. Thankfully, no one was in the set of rooms. Leila pointed to a clock sitting on a side table, reminding Carter they had to hurry.

Creeping through the closest doorway, they found a giant bed covered in candy bar wrappers and empty pizza boxes. In the next room, they found the Spider-Lady's extra sets of arms. It was in the grand master suite that Carter thought to check the bathroom. Sure enough, the bathtub was filled with stolen wallets, watches, jewelry, and more. "It looks like the booty that I saw the frown clowns trying to hide in one of the circus train cars the other night," Carter said. "The car had already been filled up, so the clowns must have brought Bosso's most recent booty here."

Leila whispered, "Just what we were looking for!"

They started digging through it. But there was no journal, no bow, no lucky lockpicks, and no wooden box. "They aren't here," Carter muttered, feeling his blood turn hot.

"Then where would they be?" Leila asked.

"I don't know," Carter fumed.

"We need to return all this stuff to their proper owners," Leila said.

"There's no way you and I can haul out this stuff without getting caught," Carter said. "We'll grab our stuff, then call the cops anonymously."

"But we saw Bosso and the gang pay off the sheriff by the pool downstairs," Leila said, simmering. "Our hands are tied." She patted the pocket of her jacket, and Carter heard the clinking of metal cuffs. "If only *their* hands were tied..." she added, gritting her teeth.

"Hey, there's one room left," Carter said and waved

for Leila to follow. The last room was locked. There was a handwritten sign taped to it that read:

STAY OUT!!
NO HOUSEKEEPING!!

"Well, that's ominous," Leila said. She pulled out her old rusty lockpicks again and went to work. A moment later, the door opened. "Holy guacamole! Look at that diamond! It's huge!"

In the center of the room was a bed covered in blueprints of a stage, yellow notepads with furious handwriting scratched all over them, and on top of it all, the world's largest diamond, the Star of Africa.

"He stole it!" Leila said. "Bosso already stole it!"

"No, he didn't," Carter said, looking more closely. "My uncle trained me over the years to spot the difference between a real diamond and a fake one. Uncle Sly always said stealing a fake was a waste of time. And this one—it *looks* real, but it's a fake."

"Then why does Bosso have a fake replica of—" Leila

didn't finish her sentence. She and Carter came to the exact same conclusion at the exact same time.

"Bosso is going to switch out this fake one with the real Star of Africa tonight at his show," Carter explained. "He's going to steal the world's largest diamond in front of everyone."

Carter thought of all the people his uncle had ripped off and of all the heartache that he himself had helped to cause. He cracked his knuckles, then said, "We have to stop him."

HOW TO...

Move Objects with Your Mind!

You've returned! I'm so pleased. I have another trick I'd like to teach you. No lollygagging—let's get to it.

They say a magician never reveals his or her secrets. Unless, that is, the magician is teaching a fellow magician. Which I am. So here's a little trick that I think you'll enjoy. It is certain to astound and astonish! (If not, you have the wrong audience.) We already know that Bosso was planning to move the giant diamond into his treasure stash. Well, this is how to move a ring WITH JUST YOUR MIND (but really with a *string*).

WHAT YOU NEED:

A button-up shirt–which is what you
should be wearing. It's always nice
to look nice on stage. Dark colors are
better; black is best.
A stick–preferably one foot (or so) long
or a wand, if you'd like
A thread–this should be about the same
length as from your shoulder to your
fingertips. It is best if the color matches
your stick or your clothing. (Bonus
points if your clothes match your stick!)
A ring–perchance one off an audience
member's finger (I'd avoid anything too
valuable.)

HELPFUL HINTS (PRACTICE!):

Have I mentioned practice to you
before? I have? Good. Let me say it
again. Practice before you perform this!
(And nap and snack...) You'll thank me
for it later.

STEPS (*BEFORE* YOU HAVE AN AUDIENCE):

1. Fasten the thread to the top of the stick.

2. Fasten the other end of the thread to a button on your shirt.

STEPS (*AFTER* YOU HAVE AN AUDIENCE):

3. Ask an audience member for a ring. If you already have one, give it to an audience member to inspect for any trickery. Then ask for it back.

4. Put the ring over the top of the stick, moving it slowly (so no one sees the thread!).

5. Move the stick away from your body *slowly*. The ring should go up. Now move the wand back toward you. The ring will go down. You now have complete control over whether the ring moves up or down the stick—simply by moving the stick back and forth!

SIXTEEN

After meeting in the lobby of the resort's main hall, Carter, Leila, Theo, and Ridley raced all the way down the hill to Vernon's Magic Shop. They didn't stop for so much as a breath of air. After they rushed through the door, Leila slammed the door shut.

"Abracadabra!" Presto squawked.

Carter and Theo fell to the floor, panting for breath. Ridley leaned back in her wheelchair and fanned herself.

"Dad...Bosso...thief...steal...diamond...tonight," Leila wheezed.

"Slow down," Mr. Vernon said, coming out from behind the counter. "Take a deep breath and start over."

The four misfits did just that. They started with their stakeout at the pool and everything Carter and Leila had discovered in Bosso's locked bedroom. The entire time, Mr. Vernon remained calm and collected. When they were done, he took a deep breath himself and said, "Well, that's disappointing of Bobby."

"Who's Bobby?" Carter asked.

"Never mind," Mr. Vernon said, perturbed. "Let's focus on one thing at a time. I told you that I would never condone what you four spent the afternoon doing."

Leila spoke up, "But I thought you said—"

"Regardless, you are armed with information that I'm sure the local law enforcement would like to know. Perhaps you should call and inform them?"

"I would but we can't—" Leila went on.

"—Sheriff Shaw is on Bosso's payroll—" Ridley added.

"—we saw Bosso pay him off—" Carter continued.

"—it looks like we're on our own," Theo finished.

"On my own? I wish!" Olly said, waving his thumb at his sister. "This one is always following me."

"Following you?!" Izzy laughed. "I came out first!

You've been following *me* around since we left Mom's womb!"

"Olly! Izzy! Where did you come from?" Leila cried.

"We wanted to see how things turned out, so we trailed you. You took off so fast, we didn't have a chance to ask if you liked our two-man show," Olly said.

"Two-*man* show? You mean, one-*woman*, one-*boy* show," Izzy smirked.

"I see your numbers have grown." Mr. Vernon smiled. He seemed surprisingly calm. Maybe even *too* calm…"You're practically an army now. It appears none of you are on your own. You remind me of my own friends when I was your age. We were unstoppable."

"What are *you* going to do, Dad?" Leila asked.

"Me? I'm going to go watch the show, of course," Mr. Vernon said. "It's important for magicians to watch other magicians. That's how we learn."

"That's it?!" Carter asked. "What are you going to do about the diamond?"

"*Me?*" Mr. Vernon asked. "I thought *you* were going to do something about it."

"We are," Ridley said. "We have a plan!"

"You do? Pray tell."

"Well, I think the four of us—" Ridley started.

"*Six* of us," Olly and Izzy interrupted.

"Fine! The six of us will stop Bosso. As for the how…" Ridley paused. Her chest sank, as if she were suddenly losing steam. "Well…I guess we only have the concept of an idea of a plan."

"Well, a *well*-executed show must be *well* thought out *well* ahead of time." Mr. Vernon grinned. "Plan carefully. No one likes a sloppy show. Feel free to use whatever you want from the shop, of course. What is mine is Leila's, and what is Leila's is yours."

"But aren't you going to help us?" Carter asked, shocked by Mr. Vernon's carelessness.

"I will be helping in my own way. After all, I trust that you six have things well in hand," Mr. Vernon said, picking up his top hat and cape. "There are leftovers in the fridge. Help yourselves. I'm going to head out for an early dinner with the Other Mr. Vernon at the hotel and then have a polite conversation with an old friend. Let's hope for the best. Either way, I suspect we'll all see a truly amazing show tonight."

Mr. Vernon turned the sign on the shop door from OPEN to CLOSED, COME AGAIN SOON. "Leila, make sure to

lock up when you leave! Ta-ta for now." Then, with
a flourish of his cape, he disappeared, and the door
closed all by itself.

"*Hrmph*," Ridley said. "I was expecting him to be a
little more...helpful."

"Me too," Carter whispered.

"This is an awful situation to be placed in," Theo
said. "We're just kids. What can we do?"

"We can do magic," Leila said.

"So can Bosso," Ridley reminded her. "And his
tricks seem *real*."

"But we have one another," Leila added.

"And Bosso has a whole gang of Sideshowers and

Pock-Pickets and frown clowns," Carter replied. "We're just a bunch of...of..."

"Misfits!" the parrot squawked.

"Rude bird!" Leila said.

Carter shook his head. "Presto is right. The Pock-Pickets were right. We're just a bunch of misfits. We can't do anything."

"Yes, we can!" Leila shouted, slamming her fist on the counter. It was the first time Carter had seen Leila truly angry. "Just because we're misfits doesn't mean we aren't amazing. In fact, I think being misfits makes us *more* amazing. Carter, you have street smarts and fast hands. I can escape from anything. Theo can make things float. Ridley is a total brainiac. And Olly and Izzy are hilarious. Plus, they know the Grand Oak better than I do. If we work together, we can stop Bosso from stealing the Star of Africa."

"But things could get sticky," Carter said. "We could get into trouble—big trouble."

"What's life without a little risk?" Leila said firmly. "But you're right. Everyone should have a chance to walk away right now. No hurt feelings. If anyone's scared or doesn't want to go up against Bosso or has homework, now's the time to say something."

The gang of misfits looked at one another in silence.

Carter thought of the past few days. He had spent his life minding his own business, letting Uncle Sly get away with all sorts of bad things. But now he had a chance to do something—not to help himself, but to help others.

"I'm in," Carter said. "I've got nothing to lose."

Theo smiled. "I have everything to lose, but this sounds like a challenge that I cannot miss."

"No one steals from me and gets away with it," Ridley said. "What about you two? You don't have a beef with Bosso."

Olly narrowed his eyes. "Bosso is a jerk and that's enough *beef* for me."

"We went up to try to talk to him after the show," Izzy explained, "since we're showbiz people too, you know? All he said was, 'Shoo, flies.' Then that Walrus guy pushed Olly."

Olly and Izzy both shook their heads in disgust.

"The only thing we hate more than a *thief*—" started Olly.

"—is *tomatoes*," finished Izzy.

Olly glared at his sister.

"What?" cried Izzy. "We *hate* tomatoes!"

"And *jerks!*" said Olly.

Izzy bobbed her head. "Oh yeah. That's what I was going to say. We're in." The twins rubbed their hands together, looking like little devils, and said, "So...what are we going to do?"

"Like Dad said..." Leila smiled. "We need a plan."

For a few seconds, they stood in silence, allowing their minds to churn.

"We're going to need all the breakfast leftovers in the Grand Oak kitchen," said Olly.

"And lots of syrup!" added Izzy.

"We're going to need to get Carter a suit with some hidden pockets," said Ridley.

Theo added, "And some props from the backstage of the Grand Oak theater."

"I know something we can do with the theater curtains," Leila said, grabbing a pencil and paper and marking down notes.

"What we need to do next," Carter said, "is share our ideas and then put it all together. Build a great big trap for the reigning heavyweight clown kingpin. And we need to act fast. We're running out of time."

SIXTEEN
BILLION

Gotcha again!

I'm sure you knew this was coming, right? You read
the Table of Contents at the beginning of the book
very, very carefully, didn't you?

You did? Oh good. That's all I needed to hear.
Paying close attention to details is very important for
a young magician.

But let's hurry and check out the Grand Oak Resort
with the rest of our group. Quickly now! We don't want
to keep anyone waiting....

SEVENTEEN

The Grand Oak was bustling with action when the misfits arrived. Hundreds of people had descended on the resort to see Bosso's big final show. Maybe they'd been drawn by talk of his big-top show, or maybe they were curious about the Star of Africa. The crowd was overwhelming, and the lines were long.

"This way," Leila said, heaving her giant backpack higher on her shoulders. All of the kids had a large pack filled with everything they needed. "We can get in using the service doors in the back."

"Nothing but the best for the Grand Oak's brightest upcoming stars," Olly said sarcastically.

"At least our fans won't attack us for autographs," Izzy joked.

"Plus, we can drop by the kitchen to pick up some of the goods for our show," Ridley added.

The six misfits made their way through the resort to the Grand Oak's Grand Theater. As they approached, Theo was the first to notice the ticket takers. "Oh no," he said. "We don't have tickets."

"Tickets, *schmickets*," Olly said. "You have something better than tickets—you have *us*."

"We know this theater like the back of our hands," Izzy said. "Follow us."

As they passed through the corridors, Carter noticed police officers at every exit. Seeing so many of them made Carter want to vanish all over again.

Inside the auditorium, the seats and curtains were all red velvet, and the walls were trimmed in gold. In the left rear corner, behind a thick column, the twins led the misfits through a hidden door behind wallpaper and wood paneling. Inside the small room was a ladder leading into the ceiling, and a long, narrow hallway, wide enough for one person, that seemed to spiral downward into darkness. "Up goes to the catwalk," Izzy noted.

"A *catwalk*?" Carter asked, wondering why a theater would need a place for cats to walk.

"It's a series of platforms that hang by cables over the stage where the crew arranges the lights and directs special effects for the performance."

"Oh, right," Carter answered, nodding slowing, pretending to understand. "A *cat...walk*."

"Down leads to the orchestra pit and under the backstage," Olly went on with a grin.

"Divide and conquer again," Ridley said. "Theo and I will head down to survey under the stage. Izzy, Olly, you take Carter and Leila and head up. We'll meet you on the other side."

As Carter followed Leila and the twins up the ladder, his palms began to sweat. He'd never been up so high. "If you're afraid of heights, don't look down," Leila said back to Carter as she crawled out onto the thin, hanging platform.

Of course, Carter immediately looked down.

Beneath them, the venue had a large balcony and

seating for almost a thousand people. From eighty feet up, all the preshow workers below looked like miniature dolls walking about.

Keep crawling forward, Carter told himself.

When they got to the other side, Carter, Leila, and the Golden siblings began to remove some of the surprises they had in store for Bosso from their backpacks. "We'll take it from here," Izzy said. "You two go ahead. We'll catch up."

Leila and Carter nodded. They crawled across the upper skeleton of the great theater. Way down in the

pit, the orchestra tuned their instruments with bursts of noise. Carefully, they passed over the wires and ropes holding up the red curtain dividing the audience from the stage. Then they crawled above the Sideshowers and clowns, who were setting up for Bosso's big show directly below.

Quietly, Leila and Carter moved toward the rear of the catwalk maze. They were about to climb down the back ladder when they heard familiar voices below.

"Bobby, listen to reason," Mr. Vernon said. He was speaking in a more serious tone than Carter had ever heard. "If you do this and get caught, you'll go to jail. And not just for a few years this time...for the rest of your life."

Carter and Leila leaned forward, just able to see Vernon and who he was talking to—B. B. Bosso.

"What's going on?" Leila whispered. "How does my dad know Bosso?!"

Carter had no idea, but a sinking feeling gripped his stomach.

"Don't act like you care about me," Bosso said scathingly to Vernon. "We haven't been friends in thirty years."

"I disagree," Mr. Vernon said. "Don't you

remember the old pledge? I still believe every word. As we said in the Emerald Ring: *'The magic of true friends is that even apart, they can't long be cut off from what lives in the heart.'*"

"Don't spout that nonsense at me. That was a lifetime ago!" Bosso growled.

"I still consider you a friend, Bobby, even if an estranged one."

"It wasn't just years that separated us," Bosso chuckled. "You always were a sentimental fool. No wonder you stayed in this wretched town."

"If it's so terrible, then why return?"

"Isn't it obvious? The Star of Africa was en route to New York City as part of its multicity tour. I could never have stolen the diamond there. But in this half-wit town, paying off all the right people was easy. As soon as I have that diamond, I'll retire. It's worth millions. I'll never have to work again."

"Don't do it, Bobby," Mr. Vernon pleaded. "Cancel the show. We'll go get a sundae at the ice-cream parlor like we did when we were kids. It's not too late. You haven't done anything wrong yet."

"No, not yet," Bosso said with a cruel smile. He snapped his fingers. "But I'm about to."

The Walrus and the Spider-Lady jumped out from

behind the curtain. The six-armed woman hit Vernon on the head with a slim silver baton, and the Walrus threw a giant canvas sack over him. "Get him ready," Bosso said. "He can take the fall for us."

Leila grabbed her mouth to stop herself from screaming. Carter reached over, took her other hand, and squeezed. He wanted to say, *Everything's going to be okay*, but he didn't want to lie.

EIGHTEEN

Carter and Leila scrambled down the ladder back-stage. They met the others in an old prop room that Bosso and his carnival crew weren't using. "What's wrong?" Ridley asked as soon as she saw the tears in Leila's eyes.

"Bosso has Mr. Vernon," Carter said.

"What?!" Olly and Izzy said at the same time.

"I think Bosso is going to frame him," Leila guessed, hugging Ridley. "They're going to make it look like my dad stole the diamond."

"What do we do?" Theo asked.

Carter thought hard before saying, "We stick to the plan."

"Forget the plan, Carter—we have to rescue Mr. Vernon!" Ridley snapped.

"*We can do both*," Carter said, a glimmer in his eye. "Remember what the carnival psychic, Madame Helga, said? *If you work together and stay true to one another, nothing will bar you.* If we stick to the plan, we can prove Bosso is the thief, and Mr. Vernon goes free. It's the best way. You're going to have to trust me on this."

The misfits were hiding backstage when Bosso's show began. The Pock-Pickets opened with the same song and dance to introduce Bosso, who then transformed roses into dandelions. "It's the exact same show he performed at the big top," Ridley noted. "No points for originality here."

Bosso went through his entire routine with gusto.

"Such a wonderful crowd!" Bosso cheered, his crooked smile the only indication that he might be hiding something. "I have shown you wonders, but it is time for something else to razzle and dazzle you. I would like to introduce you to the real star of

the show...the world's largest diamond: the Star of Africa!"

Four security guards came out with a black metal box the size of an adult man's fist. They set it on a table next to a glass podium rising several feet over the stage. When they opened the box, an "*Ooooooh*" ran through the massive audience.

Gently, Bosso picked up the diamond. A darkness twinkled in his eye.

Carter recognized the look. It was pure greed.

Misdirection was at play here, but Carter wasn't sure

which direction he should be looking. He noticed the glass podium rising several feet over the stage—there was a mechanism in it that would make the diamond vanish. It was all explained in the book Mr. Vernon had given him.

"Found in 1905, the Cullinan Diamond was presented to King Edward VII of Great Britain on his sixty-sixth birthday," Bosso said as he placed the beautiful sparkling gem on the glass podium. "It was cut into several diamonds, the largest of which is here before you: the Great Star of Africa. As you can see, there is nothing quite like it. It is beyond beauty and beyond value. It is my humble honor to include it in my show today."

The audience clapped, ready for more. "What are you going to do?" a man hollered from the middle of the audience. Carter looked over and realized that the man was Bosso's own security guard, only he wasn't wearing his creepy clown makeup anymore.

"Why, make the diamond disappear, of course!" Bosso said. The security guards seemed suddenly alarmed. "Don't worry, don't worry! I'll put it back!"

Everyone laughed—everyone except the misfits.

"Now, I'd like everyone in the audience to keep

their eyes on the Star of Africa," Bosso said. "Don't look away. Focus, focus, focus..."

Bosso pulled out a purple sheet and threw it over the diamond. Only for a second. He pulled the sheet back and the diamond was gone.

"Where is it?" Bosso smiled. "Why, all around you, of course! Look up and see the diamond dust." Silver glitter sprinkled down over the audience.

"Now, as much as I would like you all to keep it— HA!—I suppose I must bring it back...." Bosso rubbed his hands together. "Count with me, friends. On the count of three. One...two...three!"

There was a blast of flame and smoke from the podium, and the diamond appeared again, a spotlight striking it. Rainbow reflections exploded across the stage. The audience gasped and then broke into another thunderous round of applause.

"Guards, I suppose you'll be wanting this back?" Bosso said.

The four security guards walked toward the diamond. Carter squinted and noticed that some of the luster of the diamond was gone. This wasn't the real Star of Africa. This was the fake. The real diamond had been switched out during the act, just as the misfits suspected. Carter knew what he had to do.

Suddenly the lights in the entire theater went out, and the world was plunged into darkness.

"Guards! Police!" Bosso yelled in the pitch black. "Someone is stealing the diamond! Seal the doors, bar the exits, let no one leave. Wait...I...I have him!"

The sounds of a struggle echoed from the stage. There was a crash of breaking glass. People gasped in fear and excitement.

"We have him!" Bosso roared.

Conveniently, the lights came back on.

Bosso, the Walrus, and the Spider-Lady were holding a struggling Mr. Vernon facedown on the stage. The fake diamond was on the floor, mere feet away.

"We have the culprit in custody!" Bosso said to the crowd. "Police, arrest this man. He tried to steal the Star of Africa!"

Bosso, out of breath, raised his hands to the crowd. "Well, I hadn't expected *that* ending to my show. But who doesn't like a little added excitement? Crisis averted, ladies and gentlemen."

"Thanks to you!" the Spider-Lady said. "You're a hero! You stopped that wild man."

The audience cheered with approval. Bosso bowed

as people stood, clapping harder.

"I am humbled and honored," Bosso said, taking another bow. "Thank you! Thank you!"

Without inspecting it properly, the guards shoved the diamond into its black case and locked it tight. Several policemen led Mr. Vernon off stage in handcuffs.

"The show's not over yet," Carter whispered to the others. "Let's get the *real* show started...."

NINETEEN

"Let's hear it for our hero, B. B. Bosso!" Olly and Izzy said as they strolled out onto the stage behind Bosso.

Bosso seemed confused. He looked to the Walrus and the Spider-Lady, but both shrugged, just as puzzled.

"Come on, keep on clapping!" Olly shouted to the crowd.

"That's right!" Izzy added. "Give our hero a warm welcome!"

"Welcome?" Olly said. "But the show's over."

"Is it?" Izzy asked, scratching her head. "I could have sworn the show was just beginning."

"I wouldn't mind that at all," Olly said. "Who wants more?"

The crowd cheered as Bosso's fake smile began to crumble. The Walrus growled at Olly and the Spider-Lady glared at Izzy. But neither of them could do anything in front of the crowd. They backed toward the edges of the stage.

"What's wrong, Bosso? You look worried," Izzy said. "Surely you don't want to disappoint your fans."

"Of...of course not," Bosso stuttered.

"He's not worried," Olly said, poking Bosso in the belly. "He's hungry! I'd be hungry too after a show like that."

"I could use a bite to eat myself," Izzy said, taking Bosso's hand and leading him to the center of the stage. Then she pulled out an umbrella and opened it. "But I'm worried about the weather. It looks cloudy with a chance of breakfast."

Olly pulled a cord. Heaps of cold eggs, bacon, oatmeal, and bagels showered Bosso. Maple syrup dripped from above, covering him. Assuming this was part of the show, the crowd roared with laughter. Bosso's face turned red under all the oatmeal. He glanced toward the Walrus and the Spider-Lady, but they were too busy looking around the auditorium for another way out.

Olly leaned toward the crowd and bit his finger. "Oops! What a perfectly dreadful waste of a good meal!"

"Looks like someone has *egg* on their face," Izzy added.

"That's our cue," Carter said to the others behind the curtain. "Are you ready?"

Ridley, Theo, and Leila nodded.

Theo, in his tuxedo, escorted Leila and Ridley—both in beautiful matching silver-sequined dresses—out onto the stage. They tiptoed and wheeled around the spilled breakfast (and Bosso) to the front of the stage. Theo produced his violin from his jacket and a bow from his pocket. (Not his magic bow but a regular one.) "I'd like to play a tune of thanks for our hero, B. B. Bosso." Theo's jaunty melody filled the air as Leila grabbed Olly and Izzy and began a line dance. They tried to get Bosso to dance with them, but he refused, fuming. The twins spun Leila off to the side of the stage, where she rolled into the curtain, wrapping herself in it like a mummy. But when her form unrolled, it was no longer Leila—it was Carter.

Ridley held up a sign that said: APPLAUSE! The audience obliged again.

"Where am I?" Carter asked the audience. He stumbled away from the curtain in his own magician's suit, top hat, and cape. The audience clapped and laughed in response. "I'm on stage? But I have terrible stage fright!" He gave a sly wink to the enormous villain.

"You!" Bosso growled.

"Me!" Carter smirked, directing his performance toward the audience. "Bosso and I are old friends, you see. He once offered to take me under his wing. Such a generous man!"

Bosso's face was the color of angry strawberries. The Walrus and the Spider-Lady had tried to sneak away, but Olly and Izzy guided them back to center stage with Bosso.

"I'm going to murder you," Bosso whispered so only Carter could hear.

"Did you hear that, folks?" Carter shouted. "Bosso wants to make *me* vanish like he did the diamond! He should know by now: Vanishing is *my* skill."

Carter climbed onto the glass podium and bowed for the audience. When he took off his top hat, two white doves flew over the crowd. Ridley tossed the purple sheet into the air, letting it drape over Carter. By the time the sheet touched the podium, Carter was gone.

How did Carter vanish? Simple. The same way Bosso made the diamond vanish, using a drop mechanism hidden within the glass podium. When Carter stepped onto the podium, he activated its lever and fell through a secret chute. Like a superfast elevator, he moved from the stage to below the stage, with the sheet hiding his escape.

As soon as Carter found his footing, he saw the Tattooed Baby at the master light switch and the Pock-Pickets with the real Star of Africa.

"Put the diamond down!" Carter said.

"*Back for more we see, we see.*

You cannot escape; you cannot flee!

It's that kid! It's that brat!

Let's trap him like a rat!" the singers sang.

"Did you prepare that verse just in case I showed up?" Carter shivered. "That is *pretty creepy*."

The Pock-Pickets snarled. As the thieving quartet ran at Carter, he pulled a handful of marbles from his pockets and threw them on the floor. The Pock-Pickets slipped and slid, slamming into one another as they flipped into the air.

As soon as they hit the ground, Carter leapt on top of them. He pulled four sets of handcuffs from his jacket. With his fast hands, he locked one singer's wrist to another's ankle, over and over, until the barbershop quartet couldn't move.

"*We're supposed to guard Bosso's treasure,*

and now we'll be the source of his displeasure," they sang.

"*Let us goooooooooooooooo!*"

"How about *nooooooo*?" Carter sang back.

The Tattooed Baby pulled off his shirt and flexed his muscles. He ran at Carter. Carter stepped to the side at the last moment and let the baby run straight into the wall, knocking himself out. "Baby needed a nap," Carter quipped, proud of himself.

Carter grabbed the diamond and hid it in his top hat. Then he hopped on the elevator mechanism and hit the lever to shoot him back up to the stage.

A flash of fire and a poof of smoke hid his reentry. Carter now stood on the podium. Olly and Izzy were dancing in circles around a fuming Bosso as Theo played his violin for the audience.

Ridley again held up her sign saying: APPLAUSE!

Carter bowed for the audience, who cheered and whistled. Then he turned, bowing just for Bosso. When he did, he took off his top hat, letting Bosso see what he had inside.

"Want the real Star of Africa?" Carter whispered so only Bosso could hear. "Come and get it."

Then he ran to the curtain, wrapped himself up in it, and as the form uncurled, Leila popped out.

"Hello again!" she said.

"After that boy!" Bosso roared, waving for his side-show goons to follow.

Carter was backstage. As the villains closed in on him, he pulled a sword out of his sleeve. He hooked his foot into the loop of two ropes marked with a pink bow. He cut the second rope, and as several sandbags sped down, Carter flew up.

"Ta-ta." He waved to the villains.

"Get him!" Bosso growled, climbing up the nearest ladder. The Walrus went after him, but the Spider-Lady climbed straight up the rope. They all careened across the catwalks. The Spider-Lady nearly had Carter. But he pulled two decks of cards from his pocket and shot all 104 cards at her. When she tried to run after him, she slipped on the cards and nearly tumbled over the railing. The Walrus pulled her upright, then lunged forward, but Carter dodged, leaping to another platform.

Rounding a corner, Bosso reached out and snatched Carter's top hat.

When he looked inside, it was empty.

"Now you see it..." Carter said, holding up the diamond in one hand. "Now you don't!" With his other hand, he made it disappear.

Bosso, the Walrus, and the Spider-Lady had convened on Carter's catwalk. They bolted at him, hands outstretched, ready to grab him, but Carter clasped another rope that carried him gently down to the backstage below. Bosso screamed in fury, "After him!"

As Carter ran, he could hear his friends at the front of the stage, putting on what sounded like a fantastic show. Theo's music, Olly's and Izzy's dancing, and the audience's laughter buoyed his heart. "This has to work," he whispered to himself.

Now backstage, Bosso and his goons were sliding down poles from above. The Walrus landed in front of Carter, with Bosso behind him. Carter ran to the side, through another layer of curtains, and another, and another.

He jumped through a canvas painted to look like a brick wall, then ran into a real wall. Bosso was almost on him. Carter turned, ran down a short hall that made a left turn, then another left turn, then a left turn again. He came to a dead end. He turned to the side and ran through a door. It was a props closet, and there was nowhere else to go. "No!" Carter shouted.

He was trapped.

TWENTY

As Carter turned, he found himself cornered by Bosso, the Walrus, and the Spider-Lady.

"You're done, boy," Bosso said. "Give me the diamond."

Carter looked desperately around the room. There were shelves of old props, a table with an antique gramophone, musty curtains, and giant mirrors. He grabbed a baseball bat from a nearby shelf, accidentally turning the gramophone on. Instead of playing, the needle rubbed against the record as it spun, making a terrible scratching sound.

Carter swung the bat as Bosso reached for him. "Leave me alone!"

"Give me the diamond you stole!" Bosso growled.

"You stole it first!" Carter snapped.

"And now I'm going to steal it back!" As Bosso lunged at Carter, Carter swung again. Bosso backed off, but a sinister grin crawled across his face. "You're trapped, boy. Give it up and I might let you live."

"Like Mr. Vernon?" Carter said. "You framed him!"

"The old fool had it coming," Bosso spit. "Well, I've got news for him. Once the diamond is mine, I'll have everything I've ever wanted right at my fingertips. And Dante...*Goody-Boy Dante*...will be left to rot in a prison."

"Until everyone realizes you replaced the Star of Africa with a fake during your act," Carter said, swinging the bat as the Walrus and the Spider-Lady reached for him.

"By then, I'll be long gone. I'll be in Bora Bora, sipping frosty umbrella drinks and working on my tan," Bosso said.

"You're horrible, you know that? First you set up your carnival games so no one could win, then your Pock-Pickets robbed the people who came to your show, you paid off the sheriff so he'd look the other way, and now you've stolen the Star of Africa by switching it with a fake! You ruin people's lives. Admit it!" Carter demanded.

"I admit all of it! It's not my fault that the world's too stupid to realize when it's being suckered. I only show up where I know I can take advantage." Bosso's wild smirk grew on his face. "I'm an entertainer. People adore me....Will that ever make me rich enough? Hardly! But that diamond sure will! So yeah, I took it. What are you gonna do about it, kid?"

"Only everything." Carter smiled, dropping the bat on the floor. "Thank you, Mr. Bosso. That's all we needed to hear."

"*We?*" Bosso whispered.

Carter pulled a rope hidden in a far corner. The four walls and ceiling of the *fake* prop room fell away. Carter, Bosso, the Walrus, and the Spider-Lady were left standing on the center of the stage. The entire audience—cops and all—had heard everything Bosso had confessed.

"How?" Bosso screamed.

"You were chasing me backstage through curtain after curtain," Carter said. "I led you in one big circle, straight into a trap. And just in case anyone missed your confession..." Carter moved the needle back on the gramophone record and switched it from Record to Play.

"I admit all of it! It's not my fault that the world's too stupid to realize when it's being suckered." Bosso's recorded voice played back for the audience.

Ridley had been holding up a sign for the audience that said: SILENCE!! She tossed it on the floor and wheeled backstage with the others.

Then Ridley, Olly, Izzy, Leila, and Theo pushed a

line of hotel room service carts, one tied to the next, onto the stage. They removed the silver tray lids, one after the other. Each cart was heaped with the stolen goods from Bosso's bathtub: wallets, rings, bracelets, watches, wedding bands, and more.

"Police, townspeople, visitors," Carter shouted. "Bosso tried to steal the Star of Africa, but he was also working with the sheriff and a dangerous band of pickpockets. If you lost something in the last few days, it's probably here."

"He stole my wedding ring!" someone in the audience shouted.

"He stole my wallet!"

"He stole my earrings and bracelet!"

"I spent my whole allowance on his dumb games!"

The entire audience began booing him.

Two police officers took the sheriff into custody, while the rest rushed the stage and surrounded Bosso and his goons. Theo asked, "Would you like to take a final bow?"

Leila ran off the stage and over to Mr. Vernon. She hugged her dad and said, "We did it!"

"Yes, you did," Mr. Vernon said, rubbing at his bruised skull. "I never had a doubt in my mind."

"Let me take those handcuffs off," the policeman said.

"No need. I've been getting out of handcuffs since I could walk." Mr. Vernon made a peculiar motion with his hands, and the cuffs fell off. He gave them to the police officer. "Voilà!"

"Brilliant," Carter whispered.

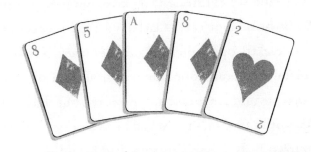

TWENTY-ONE

From the top of the stationary train car in the train yard, Carter could see the Grand Oak Resort, the quiet town of Mineral Wells, and the tents of Bosso's carnival, which was silent and still in the morning light. After everything that had happened in the last few days, Carter wondered if he was beginning to believe in magic. Not the kind where you can actually make things disappear or cast a spell, but the kind where you can't sleep because you're so full of joy that you stay awake and watch the sun come up.

Carter was certain that he'd never seen such beautiful

colors in the sky before. Sitting cross-legged on top of B. B. Bosso's "loot car," Carter watched below as the police cracked open the locks. When they finally got the metal train car door open, a mountain of wallets and watches and rings and more poured out. Later, the police would find that there had been a rash of thefts in every town B. B. Bosso's carnival had been to.

Carter and the misfits had solved hundreds, if not thousands, of unsolved petty theft crimes.

While the police collected and boxed the goods, trying to figure out how to return everything to their proper owners, Carter continued to marvel at the sky's streaks of yellow, orange, and red, all tied together like the multicolored silk handkerchiefs that his father had used in a magic trick long ago. As the brilliant sun crowned the horizon, it sent a fan of rays toward him, surrounding him with warmth.

A few tracks away, a freight train chugged off into the distance, fleeing from the rising light. Carter wondered what he would do next.

He couldn't stay at Theo's house for long. Mr. and Mrs. Stein-Meyer would only start asking questions. *Should I hop a train,* he wondered, *just to see where it takes me next?*

"You weren't going to leave without saying good-bye, were you?" Mr. Vernon asked.

"*Gaaah!*" Carter screamed, startled to find he was no longer alone. The magician sat next to him, as if he had been there the whole time. "How do you do that?" Carter asked.

"Very quietly." Mr. Vernon smiled. "Well, were you? Going to leave town?"

"I don't want to," Carter said. "But the police are already asking about my parents. I can't go into foster care. Who knows where I'd end up?"

"A wise man once said that decisions are best made in the morning after a good night's sleep, a shower, and a well-rounded breakfast. At this point, you've missed the sleep part, but the Other Mr. Vernon is making breakfast back at our home. And there are a few people who'd like to see you before you make a decision."

"Breakfast sounds good," Carter said, feeling his cheeks burn.

"Good. Come along," Mr. Vernon said as he climbed down the train car ladder.

When he walked into Mr. Vernon's dining room in the apartment above the magic shop, Carter was surprised to see the entire gang there. Theo, Ridley, Leila, Olly, and Izzy were all helping to set the table.

"Carter!" they screamed, running over to hug him.

"We did it! We really did it!" Leila said. "We took down Bosso and his circle of stooges."

"Not all of them," Theo said. "The police arrested Bosso, the Sideshowers, and the Pock-Pickets, but they never found the frown clowns."

"A worry for another day," the Other Mr. Vernon said, walking into the room with a platter stacked high with pancakes and strawberries. "For now, it's time to eat."

"Perhaps after presents?" Mr. Vernon suggested. He presented four boxes and placed them before Carter, Theo, Leila, and Ridley. "I'm sorry, Olly and Izzy, but I didn't know we'd be having two more join us."

"No worries!" Olly said, stuffing his mouth. "These pancakes are treat enough."

When the four misfits opened their packages, they found what they had thought lost—Leila's lucky lockpicks, Ridley's journal, Theo's bow, and Carter's wooden box. Carter held the small, carved box to his chest, tracing his fingers over the initials LWL. "But how?" Carter asked.

"A good magician never tells," Mr. Vernon said.

But Carter's quick mind began to sort through the details of the last few days. When he first met Mr. Vernon, he'd given Carter the book about the "vanishing object on the podium" trick. Mr. Vernon was old friends with B. B. "Bobby" Bosso. He must have known that Bosso would try to steal the diamond, and how. He also must have pickpocketed the Pock-Pickets along the way and retrieved the misfits' things.

"We were never on our own, were we?" Carter concluded. "You were looking after us from the beginning, making sure we were never in any real danger.... The coins in my pocket...? The blanket in the park...?"

Leila squinted. "What coins? What blanket?"

"I have no idea what he's talking about." Mr. Vernon smiled, helping himself to a pancake.

"What will you do now, Carter?" Theo asked.

Carter shrugged. After everything they'd been through together, after everything they'd done for him, how could he tell his friends what he'd been planning only an hour earlier? The thought made him feel empty inside. He didn't want to leave Mineral Wells or his new friends, but what other option did he have?

The others must have been able to read it all in Carter's face. "You can't leave!" Leila blurted out. "You have to stay!" Theo patted Carter on the back, and even Ridley seemed to frown.

"Actually, I may have *one* more trick up my sleeve," Mr. Vernon said. He waved the kids to follow him out of the apartment and into the connecting magic shop. Theo, always a gentleman, held the door open for everyone.

"Woof-woof. I'm a rabbit," squawked Presto.

"Silly bird." Leila laughed.

Mr. Vernon led the kids and the Other Mr. Vernon into the secret room and over to the wall covered in photos. On it were dozens of black-and-white images of different magicians. But near the bottom, there was one that stood out. It was a sepia-toned photo of six kids, their arms around one another.

"Who are they?" Leila asked, studying the photo.

"The Emerald Ring," said Mr. Vernon. "There's me as a boy, about your age, and that's Bosso. Back then he went by the name Bobby Boscowitz."

"You knew each other?" Ridley asked.

"We did. We were the best of friends," Mr. Vernon said. "Bosso, myself, and the rest of our friends were all misfits, just like you lot. But that's not what I wanted to show you. I wanted to draw Carter's attention to Lyle." He pointed to one of the boys in the photograph.

"He looks kind of like Carter," Leila said.

"Lyle was my dad's name," Carter whispered, confused.

"Just as I suspected," Mr. Vernon said, tears forming in his eyes. "From the first time I saw you, I wondered...but I decided it was impossible, that my old mind was playing tricks on me. Then this evening, when I pickpocketed the Pock-Pickets, I found your box with the initials LWL. By chance, do they stand for Lyle Wylder Locke?"

Carter nodded, stunned. "You knew my dad?"

"I did, and very well too," Mr. Vernon said. "Lyle was my cousin."

Something welled up inside Carter, forming a baseball-size lump in his throat. Other than Uncle Sly, he didn't think he had any family. "Your *cousin*?"

"When Lyle met your mother, they moved to the West Coast to be closer to her family," Mr. Vernon explained. "After your parents...you know...I knew that you ended up living with another relative, but no one seemed to know who, or where. For years, I looked for you. I never gave up, but I never imagined that fate would bring you to Mineral Wells."

"Not fate," Leila said. "Magic."

Magic, fate, or coincidence. Carter wasn't sure which was which anymore. He remembered hopping onto the yellow train car several days earlier like it was the right thing to do. Then again, all the tracks *were* leading in the same direction. Magic. Fate. Coincidence. Maybe at a certain point, thought Carter, all of these ideas start to blur together.

"Carter, would you like to come live with us?" Mr. Vernon asked. Carter didn't have any words. So he just nodded yes.

The four friends gathered in the secret room hidden inside the magic shop. After they'd gotten their faces in the local paper for saving the day, they decided they should keep practicing magic and see what they could really do.

"Should we have a name for our organization?" Theo asked.

"What about the Emerald Ring?" said Leila. "Just like my dad's group from when he was a kid?"

"That'll only make me think of Bosso and his goons," Ridley added. "Thanks, but no thanks!"

"How about the Olly and Izzy Gang?" Olly said.

"Or the Izzy and Olly Gang," Izzy said.

"Where'd you two come from?" Ridley asked, annoyed.

"You're not the only ones who know tricks," the twins said together.

Olly added, "And we're happy to join. We have our own performance to perfect, but we don't mind showing up from time to time."

"As guest stars," Izzy finished. "So yes, count us in too."

"This is awkward," Ridley said, nodding toward the twins. "But we are forming a gang of *magicians*."

"Yeah, awesome!" cried Olly.

"Does this mean we get special outfits?" asked Izzy.

Ridley shook her head. "You don't understand. You can't be in it. Neither of you know illusion work."

"That's not true!" said Olly. He grabbed Izzy's hand and tried to pull off her thumb.

"Ouch!" Izzy cried, smacking her brother.

"I think magic is about more than stagecraft," Carter said. "It's about happiness. It's about laughter. It's about that feeling you get inside. I think Olly and Izzy do that."

"Well put," Theo said, patting Carter on the back.

"I agree!" Leila said.

"Fine." Ridley gave in. "But in the future, new members will be subject to a rigorous nomination process."

"So, what are we going to call ourselves?" Leila asked.

"How about the Magical Greats?" suggested Ridley.

"The Magic Diamonds?" tried Carter.

"We need something *unique*, just like us," said Theo.

Then Carter said, "Seems like everyone's been calling us *misfits*. Bosso. The Pock-Pickets."

"I like the idea of using the bad guys' label for us," said Ridley. "That is powerful."

"Misfits," Leila repeated, trying out the word. "Nice."

"Agreed," Olly and Izzy said.

Theo gave a thumbs-up.

"The Magic Misfits," Carter said. He loved it. It was almost as if the fact that he'd never fit in was what made him belong right here at this table. "Well, now that we have our name, what should we do first?"

"Teach ourselves more magic, of course," Leila said.

Carter had learned how to do magic tricks from his uncle. But those were just that: *tricks*. There was no magic involved. From his new family and friends, Carter was learning that *real magic* did exist. You just had to know where to look.

PA GE	LI NE	WO RD
42	14	09
12	04	03
07	04	04
84	03	07
57	05	03
73	24	01
55	09	02
26	14	04
62	01	08
10	03	06
92	20	02
08	08	01
39	06	04

"— — — — — — —

— — — — — —

— — — — , — — — —

— — — — — —

— — — — — — —

— — — — — ."

HOW TO...
Read Another Person's Mind!

No! Don't go yet! The book isn't over. I have one more trick to teach you before you leave. Also, have I mentioned this is only the *first* book in the series? There are three more tales to go, each one bigger and grander than the previous. And in each, you'll learn even more magic. Dare I say by the end of this series—if you've practiced, practiced, practiced—you'll be a true magician! I'm rambling, aren't I? Where was I? Oh yes, another magic trick!

In the Magic Misfits' next adventure, they shall encounter a dangerous villain who claims to have psychic powers.

I'm not going to declare that there are—or are not—people who can actually read your mind. But I can tell you that with a little know-how, you too can learn how to READ SOMEONE ELSE'S MIND! Yes, you read that right.

Here's how to know the number that someone is thinking! You can do this with anyone and with any number. All you need are these instructions and a little math! (You may even use this to boggle your math teacher! Though he or she may say, "I told you so. . . . Math is useful!)

WHAT YOU NEED:

Paper and pencil—unless you're really good at math. You can also use a calculator!

STEPS:

1. Ask someone to think of a number. *Any number!* Make sure they write it down and put it in their pocket. (You can also do this trick over the phone.)

2. Now tell that friend to *subtract 1* from that number.

3. Have them *multiply that number by 2.*

4. Then have your friend *add their original number to that new number.*

5. Now have him or her reveal that new number to you.

**Secret magician math: Now, as quick as you can (this is where those math classes come in handy): In your head, take that new number, and add 2.*

**Second secret magician math: Then, in your head, divide that number by 3.*

6. Finally, you can announce their original number, and they will think you are AMAZING. TA-DA!

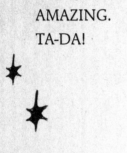

You are now a psychic—or really good at math. (Or both!) Either way, you're well on your way to being the next great magician. Now what do you need to do? That's right: *Practice, practice, practice.* (And then nap and snack and practice again. I shouldn't even have to say it at this point, should I?)

When the Misfits return, they'll be bringing more magic with them! Be ready. . . .

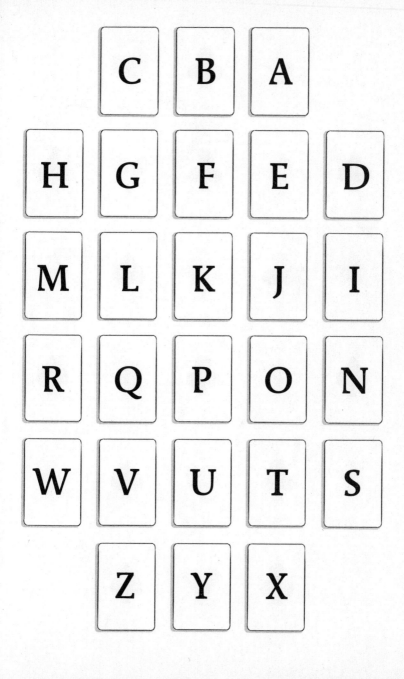

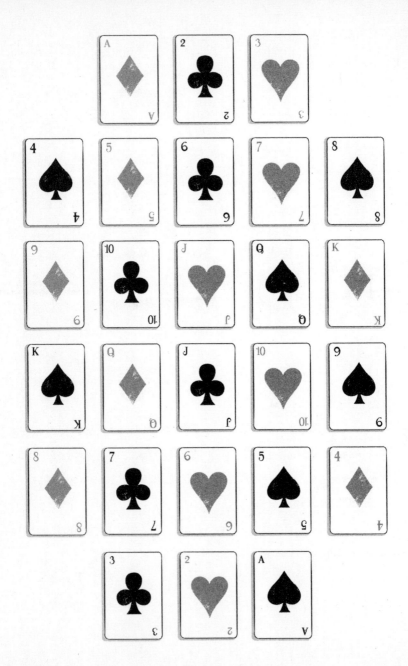

ONE LAST THING...

Hold on. Don't go. Please stay just a few moments longer.

You didn't think I'd let you close the book on Carter's tale so easily, did you? What good is any worthwhile magic show—or *story*, for that matter—without one last shocking reveal?

For my final trick, I request that you look at the previous page and...*Pick a card. Any card.*

Now concentrate on that card, very hard. Put all your energy into it. Maybe try squinting your eyes for a moment. Concentrate! With all your might! You can do it! I believe in you! *Yes! Brilliant!*

You've done it. Now, while still concentrating on your card, think back on the story you've just read. Try to remember if you've seen *your* card on any of the pages throughout this book. Go back and flip through the whole thing again. See if you can find it. I am more than willing to wait....

Did you find your card? Oh really? How *interesting*.

By now, I'm sure you've realized that what I'm playing at here is merely a bit of misdirection. You are well aware that this trick isn't about the card you picked—it is about the cards you observed while flipping through the book. What do they mean?

You clever little things noticed it was a *secret code*, didn't you? Sigh. You are much too smart for your own good.

Do you understand the cipher? Let's just say *sometimes it helps to hold things up to the light. A little illumination can often shed light on a mystery.*

Got it? Good. Now use it to decipher the hidden message throughout Carter's story.

If you've ever dreamed of being in a club like the Magic Misfits, you've probably already imagined secretly communicating with your friends. So feel free to use our card code to create your own messages too! Simple. Easy peasy!

That's all I have for you now....Why don't you take a break? Go outside and run around. You probably have time before your dinner (or breakfast) is ready. Until next we meet: Be well, be clever, and most important, be magical.

Oh, and don't bother looking for any *other* secrets hidden in the pages of this book. You certainly won't find any...*or will you*?

_ _ _ _   _ _ _ _ _ _ _   _ _ _
_ _ _ _ _   _ _ _ _ _,
_ _ _ _ _ _ _ _:
_ _ _ _ _ _ _   (_ _ _ _ _
_ _ _ _ _ _ _),
_ _ _ _ _ _ _ _   (_ _   _ _ _ _
_ _ _ _ _ _),
_ _ _   _ _ _ _ _ _ _ _ _ _ _ _
(_ _ _ _ _ _ _   _ _ _ _ _ _ _
_ _ _ _   _ _ _ _ _   _ _ _ _).

ACKNOWLEDGMENTS

Special thanks to the following carnies who ran away to join my circus: Rex "the Ringmaster" Ogle, Laura "the Lion Tamer" Nolan, Zoë "the Mentalist" Chapin, Dan "the Ventriloquist" Poblocki, Lissy "the Tattooed Woman" Marlin and Kyle "the Tattooed Man" Hilton, Damian "the Magician's Assistant" Acosta, Shea "the Strong Man" Martin, Chelsea "the Mistress of Promotion" Hayes, David "the Bull Handler" Burtka, and all the Gandy Dancers at Little, Brown, especially Megan Tingley, Karina Granda, and Alvina Ling.

Lastly, thanks to the staff at Fool's Paradise, the magic shop I went to when I was a kid. Its doors have long since closed, but its secrets will stay with me forever.

And lastly lastly, to Ed Alonzo, my own personal Mr. Vernon and the original Misfit of Magic.

Turn the page for
a magical sneak peek of

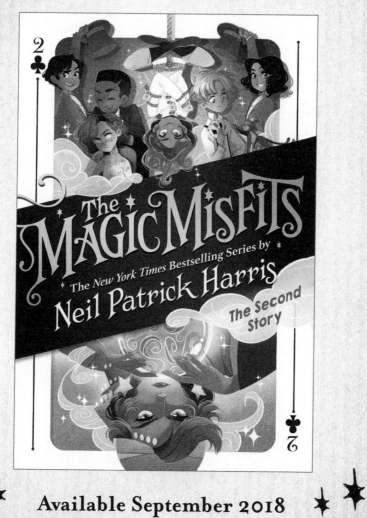

The **MAGIC MISFITS**

The New York Times Bestselling Series by

Neil Patrick Harris

The Second Story

Available September 2018

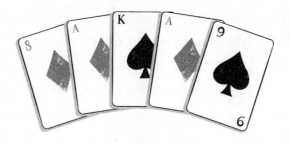

ONE

Leila Vernon did not always live in Mineral Wells. In fact, her name had not always been Leila Vernon. When she stayed at Mother Margaret's Home for Children, Leila's last name had been *Doe*.

Doe was not a name that she'd been given by family—*Doe* was Leila's name because no one knew who her family was. When Mother Margaret first found Leila, a notecard in the bassinet stated only her first name and birth date. Leila never let this get the better of her. In fact, she tried harder than the other girls to keep a positive attitude, even when they treated her as if she were as worthless as a wooden nickel.

That was why, one afternoon, when several girls from Mother Margaret's Home were dragging Leila Doe down the hallway toward Mother Margaret's office, Leila let out a loud and boisterous laugh. "Ha-ha-ha!" she shouted as they pinched her arms. "That tickles!"

Leila was not *actually* tickled by what the mean girls were doing to her, but she figured that maybe an adult would hear her loud cries and intervene. She didn't need to be psychic to know what the girls were up to, as they locked her in the darkest closet in the whole orphanage at least once a week. All because the tallest of the bunch had decided at some point that she didn't like Leila always smiling and being cheery.

The tall girl wished for Leila to be as miserable as she was. And so she and her friends went out of their way to torment Leila every chance they got. Leila fought with every breath to not show them how much they were hurting her, especially on this particular afternoon, when a group of *real-live magicians* from the town of Mineral Wells was going to perform for all the

children. Leila had been looking forward to the show
for weeks.

"Come on, guys!" Leila said with a forced smile.
"Let's all go down to the recreation room. Everyone
is probably waiting for us. There might even be cookies!"

The only response she got was a twisted echo of her
last statement. "*There might even be cookies*," the tall girl
repeated snidely. The others cackled cruelly.

As the gang dragged Leila toward Mother Margaret's office, she dug her heels into the linoleum. But
together, the girls were too strong. The soles of her shoes
left black streaks across the gray tile floor. The tallest
girl flung the office door open, and the others yanked
Leila through the room toward the familiar closet door.
They threw her into the closet and slammed the door
shut, drowning Leila's vision in darkness. Leila heard
the door lock from the other side.

"Okay, joke's over, let me out!" Leila begged,
banging on the door. "Don't you want to see the magicians?"

"Sure we do!" called one of the girls through the
thick wood. "That's where *we* are headed right now."

"Come join us...if you can!" called another. Laughter rang out like the cries of crows that often sounded across the playground outside. Their footsteps faded as they ran away.

Leila knew what would happen when she tried the knob, but—always hopeful—she tried it anyway.

It was locked. And she was alone. Again.

Leila swiveled her head back and forth, but the dark was so complete her eyes didn't register any movement. Her heart thundered as it usually did whenever the gang of girls shoved her in here. The acrid smell of the damp wooden walls stung her nose.

In the past, it had taken an adult an hour or more to discover Leila cowering in the corner of the closet. And whenever they *did* find her, they scolded Leila as if she had locked herself in the headmistress's closet.

To calm down, Leila imagined herself as a beautiful girl who was part of the magic show downstairs: purposely shut inside a cabinet on stage, then wowing the audience by disappearing without a trace, with a flash and a bang and a *whizzz-zup!*

Frustration clenched her body. The magic show was the only thing she'd been looking forward to recently. She wanted to see white doves fly from the formal jackets of the magicians, flower bouquets appear from thin air, playing cards float up and out of a deck....

Leila decided she was *not* going to allow those girls to ruin this for her. For the first time, she'd stand up, *really* stand up to them. But before she could do that, she had to figure out a way to escape.

Leila felt around in the dark, pushing her finger against the keyhole. Perhaps there was a way to unlock it from the inside. Leila had never picked a lock before, but she'd read about heroes doing it in stories. First, she'd need some tools. She plucked out the bobby pin holding her hair in place and stuck it in the keyhole. She turned it back and forth. Inside the lock, the tool met the tumblers. She heard them clinking. But without another pin, she wouldn't be able to catch them and turn the locking mechanism.

She didn't have another bobby pin. But she was standing inside Mother Margaret's *office* closet. Sweeping the floor with her fingers, her heart sped up as she encountered a lone paper clip. Luck was on her side!

She unfolded the clip. She stuck the tip into the keyhole and felt around, putting tension on the plug, seeing how far it would give. The pins clicked against the tumblers but kept slipping.

A muffled cheer came from the floor below. The show had begun.

"No, no, no!" Leila whispered to herself. In her mind's eye, she pictured the mob of magicians standing on stage, pulling rabbits out of hats, transforming marbles into pearls, levitating chairs, and flipping black silk cloaks over their shoulders. She'd been counting on some magical memories to get her through the next few months with a smile on her face.

The more she rushed, the harder it was to

manipulate the pin and clip in the keyhole. Minutes ticked by, until it felt as though she might never escape. She worried the show would end before she broke out. Leila was about to throw down her tools in frustration when she felt a distinct *click*, and the door swung open a crack. She tapped her feet excitedly against the floor in a celebratory dance.

At the top of the stairwell, a voice sounded from below: "And now for our final act..." The sound of clapping grew louder as Leila raced halfway down, then paused. In the rec room, several rows of chairs were arranged around a platform, upon which sat a distinctive man in a black suit and a tall top hat. A black cape fell from his shoulders, and when he moved his arms, a red silk lining winked at her. The man's hair was pure white and made of curls, while a straight black mustache smirked from the top of his lips. Leila plopped herself onto a middle step and watched the man with the curly white hair through the rickety wooden balusters.

You must already know who the man with the curly white hair is...but Leila didn't. This was the moment she saw Mr. Vernon for the very first time, and the sight took her breath away. Do you remember when

Carter first encountered Mr. Vernon? It was on the night that Carter arrived in Mineral Wells. He came down from the train yard to blend in with the crowds at Bosso's circus. Mr. Vernon's deft skills—flipping two coins around and around between his knuckles—blew Carter's mind.

Now, as Leila watched this same man's two assistants tie him tightly to a metal chair, she felt something even more profound than Carter had. She was certain that she'd escaped from the closet upstairs so that fate would allow her to see this man.

The stage assistants' faces were covered with a thin black stretchy fabric. First, they cuffed the man's ankles to the chair's legs. Then they wrapped a long chain around his torso and the chair's back, so that his arms were pinned to his sides. The orphans in the audience gasped as the assistants attached a thick padlock to the ends of the chain, which hung in the center of his chest. When they slipped an oil-cloth sack over the man's head, several of the children cried out in fear.

Mother Margaret stood and waved her arms. "Mr. Vernon is a professional!" she said. "Do not be alarmed!"

The man's voice came from under the hood. "*Do* be

alarmed!" he corrected. "For if I haven't freed myself by the end of this very minute, I shall run out of oxygen." Mother Margaret looked sheepish as she sat back down, as if thinking she'd made a mistake inviting this man to possibly perish in front of her wards.

Leila clung to the balusters, peering through like they were the bars of a cage. The two assistants held up a large white sheet before draping it over Mr. Vernon's body. The sheet covered him from head to toe. One of the assistants brought out a large hourglass timer, then set it down on the floor so that everyone could watch as the sand slipped through, second by second by second.

Leila held her breath. The figure under the sheet wriggled and writhed. The clanging of the clasped chains rang through the room. She couldn't help but think of herself trapped in the closet upstairs minutes earlier.

As the final grains poured into the bottom of the hourglass, the children chanted, *"Five! Four! Three! Two! One!"* The figure under the sheet grew still. Seconds passed. The audience stood, a few at a time, jaws agape, wondering if this was all part of the trick.

Leila cried out, "Take off the hood! Someone help him!"

Frantic, the two assistants raced back onto the stage. They raised the sheet, held it up before the seated man, and peered cautiously behind it. Turning to the audience, they shook their masked heads, as if to say, *We're too late!* The orphans went wild, some screaming, as the assistants dropped the sheet to the floor.

The chair where Mr. Vernon had been seated was empty!

The room erupted in gasps of surprise until one of the assistants turned to the audience and removed his mask. As soon as the pure white curls sprang out from beneath, Leila knew that they'd all been had. The magician *did* escape—and in the most unexpected way. The crowd cheered as if someone had just announced that all of them were being adopted that day.

The man with the curly white hair stepped to the edge of the stage, grinned, then took a long bow. Leila was so floored she nearly slid down the stairs. Instead she stood and clapped harder and longer than anyone else.

When the applause ended, Leila pushed her way through the crowd, elbowing the tall girl and her gruff goons aside, to approach the man. "How did you do that, Mr. Vernon?"

His eyes lit up when he saw her face. He paused as if lost in a trance, then answered quietly, "I'll bet you know exactly why I *cannot* tell you."

Leila thought hard. "A magician never reveals his secrets?"

The man chortled. He tapped her forehead lightly. "A bit psychic, are you?"

"Not that I know of," said Leila, rubbing at the spot where he'd touched her. She felt the other orphans pushing in from behind her. She fought to block them out of her mind. "Were you really in danger?"

"Oh, but I am *always* in danger," he said with a wink.

Leila laughed. "I want to learn how to escape like you did."

"I see." He squinted. "Well, it takes years of practice. Is that something you'd be prepared to do?"

"Oh yes! I'd practice *every* minute of *every* day to be like you!"

"Well, enthusiasm is rarely a bad thing," he said, considering. "What is your name, dear?"

"Leila," she answered quietly.

"*Leila*," he echoed. "How pretty! And how long have you lived here with Mother Margaret?"

"All my life."

He was quiet for a moment. "I'd like to come see you again, Leila. Would that be all right?"

Leila's face flushed. "It'd be more than *all right!*" she exclaimed. "Maybe you can teach me a trick or two?"

"Maybe..." He grinned again, the corners of his eyes crinkling with amusement. With both hands, he pinched his fingers together. As he moved his hands apart, Leila noticed that he held a soft white rope between them. He dropped one end and lowered the rope slowly into her outstretched palm. "For you. See what you can do with this. Might I suggest learning different types of knots? They can be helpful in many situations."

Leila's face flushed a deeper pink. She wanted to throw her arms around his neck and say thank you, but she didn't want to make him think she was a weirdo.

At that moment, the other orphans crowded forward, asking for Mr. Vernon's autograph and edging Leila away. She didn't mind. He was going to come back and see her again. He'd teach her a trick. *Maybe.*

She'd be ready. She'd have some new knots to show him in response.

Later, in the bedroom she shared with five other orphans, Leila pulled a tin box out from a hiding place behind a brick in the wall beside her bed. She opened the lid, revealing a few loose, glittering keys.

One key was very special to her. You see, when someone placed Leila on the doorstep of Mother Margaret's Home as an infant, they'd wrapped her in a blanket and left a string looped around her neck, with a key tied to it like a pendant. Of course, Leila didn't remember any of that; she knew the story only because Mother Margaret had shared it with her. It was this first key that'd made Leila start looking for spare ones, or ones that appeared to be lost. She hoped that someday she'd have an interesting collection of all shapes and sizes.

Staring down at her keys, Leila thought about the magic show and how Mr. Vernon had managed to break out of those impossible chains. For the first time, she felt like she'd unlocked something inside herself: a wish to escape. *Really* escape.

When the man with the white curly hair returned later that week with his husband, offering to adopt her, her wish came true—like magic.

ABOUT THE AUTHOR

Neil Patrick Harris is an accomplished actor, producer, director, host, and author. Harris served as president of the Academy of Magical Arts from 2011 to 2014. He lives in Harlem, New York, with his husband, David, their twins, Gideon and Harper, and two hilarious dogs named Watson and Gidget. *The Magic Misfits* is his middle-grade debut.